Playing Possum

Kevin Davey

Playing Possum

Kevin Davey

AAAARGH! PRESS

Published in Great Britain in 2017 by
Aaaargh! Press
119 Woodbridge Road
Ipswich
Suffolk
IP4 2NJ
United Kingdom

ISBN: 978-0-9573635-8-8

Typesetting and design by Paul Anderson.

I see quotations as outrunners on
either side of a galloping shafthorse

Sergei Eisenstein

Has to. Wants to. Six years later, in a confession of sorts, Thomas will say that any man might kill his wife.

That will be long after his blooding tonight.

– Flicks or skitter? Screen or skank?

– Both I think, don't you?

He and Fanny visit a newly opened picture house in Chelsea. They spend an hour in Hammersmith's Palais de Danse. Cajoled to the sprung floor by the jabbling horns of a jazzboat orchestra, the couple shimmy through chinoiserie. Blasts of negro trombone assault the lacquered pillars. Paper lanterns glim to ragtime sax. Table candles glow in southern scat. A hothead camera tracks their onestep lap by lap.

Don't give the rhythm meaning, she laughs. We're here to get away from that.

A clarinet percolates in copperplate, copulates in puckered bass. Let's dance perk perk, all night purple perk, our last purple erkle, not so fast pokle okle.

In truth it is Fanny who frisks: with powdered and fawning instructors, with captains stalking bored spouses, with bachelors foraging for solvent quiff. In fact with any floorflusher who is bold enough to ask for a caper. Of which there are many.

– They're decent men Tom. In the main. Decent men who enjoy dancing.

Thomas looks on from a table with a feigned grin, sipping gin and smoking. These freedoms, that tolerance, are the price he pays for their marital truce.

– May I?

– Shall we?

– Yes, yes, let's.

When she returns to her seat, Fanny is euphoric.

– That man's eyes were divine Tom. As for his trot, it was positively sinful.

The quarrel starts soon after they return home to an apartment in Crippence Court Gardens, a mansion block not far from Baker Street.

Fanny complains, as she often does, that her nerves are bad.

– My nerves are bad.

– I'll pour you a quencher, Fan. Then I must work. I've still got a Letter from London to write for McDollar, the new editor at the *Exchange*.

– More tap-tap-tapping into the small hours? While I shiver in bed, solo mi alono?

– I'm sorry.

– Are you sure that's what you'd rather be doing?

– I'm afraid I must.

– Tap-tap-tap dink. You had the same excuse at sacktime yesterday.

Last night Fanny heard bees, possibly hornets, nesting beneath the bed.

– I tried to finish, Fan. I drew a blank.

– What about me Tom? When do I get some attention? You've had nothing to say since lunchtime. Zero, zilch, zip. I've been getting the absent treatment from you the whole day long.

– I'm sorry. The *Exchange* pays well. I'm late already as you know.

– And I'm the runner up, as usual. So, Tom. Tell me. What did you think of the film?

Within minutes they were arguing about *The Idle Class*, the latest from Charlie Chaplin. When it comes to cheeky Charlot, Fan's a fan.

– Oh no we're not married he said. Haha! It was hilarious.

The house coughs on a nimbus of smoke cloaking the stalls. A fat man in a kilt knocks the Tramp down with a panto punch. He crouches over the floored clown, the feeblest of kinema foes. Chaplin half rises, the kilt readies a fist. Chaplin flattens. Rises, fist, flattens. Rises, fist, flattens. Hints at rising, fist, hoots of laughter.

– That isn't what happened.

– Sure it did. You don't believe my eyes?

– The flick was entertaining Fanny, I admit that. My thoughts about it are something altogether different. You can have my opinion, but I don't think you'll like it.

– You, Tom, separating thought from feeling? My what a turn up!

– The incidents, in themselves, were trite. A splash, a misunderstanding, a chase. The usual fare. The jester less fortunate than his audience.

– Go on.

– Rhythm and gesture, they redeemed the film. Chaplin is Hollywood's chief engineer. He understands ritual. He electrifies where once there was only gas.

– Is that all?

– Consider the tramp as the lamb, or the frailty of man, the sinner in us all.

– Well, whaddya know. Lordy be praised. The parson's in the house.

– Chaplin borrows from the liturgy to buy laughs. He's tapping the wellspring of European drama, purloining the life of Christ, peeling away the solemnity. He's Charlie the Chaplain really.

– It's a bloody comedy Tom.

– His clockwork motion is a warning that our lives are becoming automatic. That we are losing something.

– He picked up those gags in the music hall. It's entertainment, Tom. A laugh.

– Chaplain Charlot owes the church a debt that he will never repay.

– Spoken like a true banker.

– It's a debt of a different order Fan. You know what I mean.

– Here's to your daylight Old Lady. Cheers.

Fanny burbles another gin into her glass. Thomas picks up a book with boards dressed in epic blue, a Greek flag fresh as the sky in which it kites. An advance copy from Paris. He slits its uncut pages open. Fanny swirls the liquid in her glass. She looks at the wallpaper, floral, then at framed photographs of stern in-laws, at her deco bracelet – blank eyes of pearl in silver – then back at her husband. The lid of the new book flaps and falls as Thomas carves. The volume unfurls.

– The job at the bank does pay the bills, Fan.

– Don't I know it, dull husband, my munificent benefactor.

– You didn't want me to quit.

– Not for a pittance, no I don't.

– If the new journal gets backing, gets off the ground.

– There are times, Tom, when you're a pompous bore. You laughed all the way through the film! You enjoyed the slapstick just like everyone else. When the golfer plunged into the pond you roared. And you definitely showed an interest in that waitress at the Palais.

– Fan.

– That slapper attracted your interest at double the base rate, didn't she? Mister banker with the ogling eyes. It wasn't the liturgy you were thinking of when you watched that trollop bending to clear the next table.

– Fanny, please.

– More like the breasts of the Virgin. The firm buttocks of her seat of faith. You never ever look at me like that Tom. Not anymore.

– That's not true Fan.

– You're the sneeriest snob of a man I've ever known. The coldest cod on the slab. A codling and snob that's what you are. Praise be to Tom codling the snob.

– Fanny, please stop.

– Tom codling the snobling.

It's a period piece, more or less. Put a plate on the gramophone, Second Hand Rose or Jolson bellyaching over a muscle mislaid. Add more coal to an open fire that's taking in the hearth. Find a tray, electroplated, arrange a silver teapot, jug and china cups upon it. Place the salver on a lace tablecloth. Source a hardwood dining table, chullo chullo, or fabric, tray and tea will crash to the floor. That's it. Select a date in 1922, the second quarter of the year. Insert it in a telegram or, better, beneath the masthead of a newspaper. Create headlines. Plan for a British Broadcasting Company, Birth of the Irish Republic. Chaplin back in Lambeth. Formation of Union of Soviet Socialist Republics. That kind of thing. Gandhi arrested. Railways returned to rightful owners. The hooves of horses should tick quickly through the street below, outpacing the clock on the mantelpiece. There are more props in the cupboard by the door.

Or take Tom's advice and have the scene arrange itself.

– Quarrels between them, I gathered, were not infrequent.

– The neighbours reported rhythmic grumbling.

Thomas takes a deep breath. He holds on to it with his eyes closed. He will not retaliate. He is not going to bring up Fanny's dance partners. He won't mention the tip she gave, a full florin, to the Valentino lookalike teaching coon tango. As if.

– There's one thing you must always remember, brother in law of mine.

– What's that?

– Never, no, don't ever, fan the flames of fiery Fan.

Thomas beams at his wife.

– Fanny, darling, I didn't even notice her. You are the most adorable woman I have ever seen. That's why I married you.

– Save your banana oil, Tom. I know you think I'm your biggest mistake.

– That's not true.

– Sure, there's no slip-slop. You're leer with no action. Little dicky dandler isn't dunked outside your head. But you don't fool me. That impersonal intelligence you spout about. The goggle-eyed prurience of it! It's a shilling sensation on the sly. Escape from emotion? Kiss my butt mister Harvard Sorbonne smartypants of Oxford.

– Fanny, don't do this please.

– Impersonality. It reeks like a billy goat in a library. You nibble away at Vittoria rusk, Annabella cracker, and all the other biscuits in the Jacobean bookcase. Why don't you nibble me? Frit little Tom timid as a mouse, stale crumbs littering the desk, a sprinkle on your pants.

– Fanny, please. Stop.

The squabble babels into a full-on row. The particulars don't matter a tick till Fanny leaps up from the daybed.

– You utter bastard, Tom. You wilt, you geld, you brokedick excuse for a man.

No matter who you marry, you wake up with someone else. Why hadn't he listened?

– Sometimes I wanted to escape from the whole thing and run away.

– I'm not surprised. Brace yourself.

In screen six of the shopping mall cinema the underfloor sound system is quaking. A sensory effects kit channels the momentum of Fanny's advance, the beating of a detuned piano – rapido, ruvido, relentless – through the soles and selfmoulding seats, the armprops and the embedded speakers of this evening's cosseted house.

Up pops a title card, old school and unexpected, hogging the screen for a count of six.

THE INCITING INCIDENT

Fanny towers over Thomas. His signature odour, tobacco and hair slick, cascades from the aromashower in the auditorium ceiling. Her nostrils suck and flare. As Fanny raises her right hand, her shoulders unlock and her chest swells.

Tightly sheathed in a satin tube – handrolled in Chelsea by a modish seamstress – her flapper stem busts with anger. The cramping sidelacer beneath her dress is about to split. Cotton stitches tear the stretching silk.

She changes her mind. The music stops. Instead of hitting her husband she palms his temple up from the blue book, contemptuously.

Her bracelet chips loudly against his glasses.

Thomas leaps to his feet.

A neighbour, exasperated by the yelling, bangs on the dividing wall.

– Do you hear that?

Thomas grips her forearms. She la-a-a-a-aughs.

– You are embarrassing us again. We will be asked to leave. Stop this now.

He shoves her away, turning back to his blade and his book.

Fanny staggers. She topples backwards like a skittle then floorwards, striking the wall with the back of her head.

The angry neighbour's fist and Fanny's head slam at an identical spot, exactly four feet above the skirting board and fifteen inches in from the back right hand corner of the sitting room. Her skull and his fist drum at precisely the same moment, sandwiching her papery scalp and bobbed brown hair, the green floral wallpaper, an uneven seam of dried glue-size reinforced at points with dabbed molasses, a layer of coarse cracking plaster, a curtain of discoloured London stock baked from clay scraped from Kent and seamed with lime-based mortar, a recto coating of finer plaster, almost flawless, and two matt skins of rich white paint the top coat of which is being gouged and furrowed by the rim of a silver pinkie ring, Danish in design. Exploding tilth dusts the bonespread skin of a freckled paw which pounds and pounds.

The left hand of the picture house pianist tolls harsh chords with the same doomed tempo. Each knell, each clang, each brash slambang synchronises with the neighbour's fist. Clawhammer fingers clout into the keyboard.

Keys, paw, fist, claw, pounding, resounding, boom upon boom through the apartment room and the gilded gloom of the cold and recently converted music hall.

At the parietal rap, a red spray of sap spurts slo-mo through Fanny's hair.

This morning a cupboard masking the smear was removed by police officers and returned to its original spot in the bedroom. A medical expert from St Mary's determined the exact point of impact of Fanny's head among the blockprint blooms. A chalk circle was drawn around the spot.

– So low?

– Not much higher than my elbow.

– How tall was the victim?

– Tall sir?

– Just find out man.

Due to the strict coincidence of time and place, the neighbour had not heard the bounce of breaking bone rebounding.

– It was a little after half past six. The argument started as my husband and I were listening to the third of four quartets on the wireless.

– The third of four, madam?

The evidence my wife gave to the coroner allowed the exact time of the incident to be established. She was able to identify the precise passage in the broadcast which had been violated by yells from next door.

– The shattered lobsterpot.

I watch, wideyed, as the catastrophe unfolds.

Fanny's shoulders slump down the wall as she flops to her left. Her flooding hair is the frothing toe of a falling paintbrush. She curves a swatch, a vivid swatch, a mortal smear, a stunning arc of gore towards the floor. As she sinks Fanny grasps a bookcase to her right, straightening a little. The bloody curve gains a stem. Her head nods as she reaches the floor. She straightens her neck slowly, with difficulty, to look across at Tom. A final dab appears just above the skirting board.

How the old stories sneak up and impose themselves, time and time over again.

– We need a trumpet on the soundtrack there.

The director snaps his instructions from a couch at the back of the edit suite.

– Locke met a blind man who said scarlet sounds like a trumpet. Try a long sustained blast. No. No, use a barely articulated note, breathy and faltering, pfthherrrrrrthhhh. Fade it to nothing before she hits the floor, somewhere like, ah, fourth flower down. Fuck it. Do both. Give me some other options too.

The intern nods, indexes the shot and keys in the task.

– A trumpet? Now I will show you what must happen hereafter.

I continue to beat the wall to the right of my laptop.

– Drunken bastards, drunken selfish bastards, row after row, night after bloody night.

A tower of books topples from my desk, nine-elevened by my elbow.

– Heraaarghhuhuhuhhuhooo

An elderly man in the stalls behind me starts to chortle. His laughter, which I hadn't expected to spark this early, spreads through the cinema. It's too soon, far too soon.

Grigson said he never heard Tom laugh. I'm guessing Grigson was a bore.

A few feet from my desk, greek blue in one hand, a blade in the other, I watch Tom hook his arms through fallen Fanny's pits.

– Fan. Speak to me. Fan. Damn!

As Thomas lifts his wife his knees, and then the knuckles of his pelvis, slip and scuff against the satin dress that bunches at her shoulder blades. Fanny's calves are exposed, then her kneecaps. The hem insists on rising. The camera tracks its progress. A gratuitous shot, the critics say. What do they know! Femmes fatales played a walk-on part but cinema would never have got to its feet without vulnerable snatch. Lillian Gish unconscious and drifting on an ice floe towards a waterfall. Alla Nazimova, consumptive and wilting, in Camille. King Kong's kidnapped bride Fay Wray. Hollywood was built, very deliberately, on the frailest of foundations. Conscious of the tradition or not, Fanny pays her dues. The shot stays.

As Thomas hauls Fanny's inert body back into the centre of the room, her poll lolls across his paunch. His wife's blood guilts his shirt and tags the lining of his jacket.

His face upturned, his wife's body hanging like a sacrifice from his crooked arms, the blade and the book both raised high, Tom is the spit of a priest calling on a pagan deity, Mayan let's be sayin', at a weekend masquerade in a Bloomsbury bolthole.

– God help us. Come on Fan.

Our loftier neighbour in Crippence Gardens has never been seen on the stairs. We've heard a rumour he's a copper with stripes, a pal of the landlord. The chief proof for his existence is the steady pad above our heads as he patrols the ceiling at night, along with a terminating stamp just before each turn. A uniform drops by occasionally. As far as we can tell the cop without a countenance receives no mail. We don't even know his name.

Be personal, you must be personal, or else it's no good.

– Almost there darling. Here we go.

Thomas drops his wife on to the daybed. She is trying to speak. Setting the blue book down on a table in the centre of the room, he crouches beside her.

– Fan, talk to me.

– Yoob. Yooble.

– Are you all right?

– You bully.

– Fanny.

– Thug.

– No. Fan, please.

– Murderher.

Startled, Tom straightens up, taking a step backwards.

There is no market for talking pictures. That's the majority view at the studio. Synchronisation will never be achieved. Talkies will ruin the great beauty of silence.

– Pictures, real pictures, are pantomimic.

– There would be nothing left to the imagination.

Fanny's mouth is a fountain of false accusations. Tom's ear receives.

A word, once spoken, cannot be wiped out.

Silently revolving the knife in his hand, Tom eyes his reflection in the glinting blade. Pompous. It is furbished that it may glitter. Parson. The tip of his thumb tempts the edge. Codling.It is sharpened to make a sure slaughter.

He looks down at his wife. His eyes close. Seven then eight.

I will guide his raging hands.

Gouges, thrusts, deep and bloody. A moment of madness, he will tell the court. Stabs, frenzied. Fanny's screams are little more than helpless yelps. Slash, slit, gash. I conceal nothing; I make no excuses. Sharp glissandos rip through the sitting room, tear at the stalls.

– The craving for melodrama is perennial, isn't it?

– It must be satisfied.

– That was a corker.

– Slash movies suck. In my opinion they're all the same.

The psychotherapist appointed by the court called it an example of Sebastian's Revenge, a recently identified syndrome in which the formal and erotic anxieties of aspiring artists intensify and are redirected, with varying degrees of violence, at those who trigger them. She advised the judge that in Tom's case voluntary incarceration and treatment would be more effective than a prison sentence.

– In your report you say that the accused had sought out paintings of St Sebastian in Bergamo, Paris and Venice. And that he had spent considerable amounts of time inspecting them.

– That's true. The signs were there. They were overlooked at the time.

– In Paris he attended Annunzio's Martyrdom of St Sebastian? An infamous performance I believe?

– Yes. With hindsight we can see an obsession was forming.

– He also wrote an unbalanced poem in which he put himself in St

Sebastian's shoes. It contained vicious lines. 'Love me because I have strangled you' and 'I love you the more because I have mangled you' or words to that effect, did it not?

– It did.

– That's enough. Does the prisoner have anything to say?

– I will not be treated as a case of diminished responsibility.

– Do you realise what's at stake here Mr Stern?

Let's dance perk perk all night purple perk our last purple perkle.

Sixty miles away an electrical technician, a browncoated gaffer employed in the motion picture industry, is leaving the Duke of Cumberland hotel in Whitstable. Earlier that afternoon a telegram – T departs 8pm away until Sat F – had summoned Charley Roscuro of Artistic Pictures back to the capital.

– A wonderful dancer, darling. Healing hands, they say.

– A rat too, no doubt.

– Don't be like that, Tom. You agreed not to be.

Mr Slawson, the manager of the hotel, thinks the leave-taking Londoner's half crown for the maid is excessive. The wink he gave her was unseemly. He turns to the desk assistant.

– We don't want him back. And keep an eye on that bint.

The assistant manager nods. He inks a note on the back of an index card. On the front, surname, title, domicile are set in looping script between blue rules. Red verticals store dates and payment. The back is used for quirks and estimated worth. He lodges the record in a tightly packed drawer wrestled from a scratched oak cabinet. Mr Conan introduced queues of card – one file for the guests, another for staff – when he took the position in January 1902. On his first pay day he celebrated with brandy and the inaugural issue of the Literary Supplement to the *Times*. The catalogue of guests has expanded to more than one thousand entries. Four mounds of bookish newsprint understudy his windowsill. He has spent more than twenty years compiling details of transitory guests, transient staff and authors immortal. Heaving drawers and rising stacks track his bachelor years.

– That's big data in an early form.

– Each new card, every new entry, modifies the average length of stay and spend. It adds to the pattern. It confirms custom, it creates new combinations. Each new booking amends every booking that went before it. Every reservation is changed by the act of being registered alongside others.

– Conan is the curator of the hotel's memory.

– The past is altered by the present, the present by the past.

– Can you mine index cards?

– Shuffling, that's what cards are for.

I look out of my window towards the rear of the Duke, a late Victorian wedge that splits the high street. There wasn't a card for Tom in the cabinet. Did Conan's hand tamper with the evidence? Conan wasn't part of the original investigation at all. Sergeant Winchell didn't question him.

I also believe the importance of the telegram has been overlooked. The lighting engineer referred to the cable in his testimony at the first trial. He died before the second. The Post Office confirmed its content. The exact time of delivery was verified by the young man who cycled to the hotel with the cable. He had paused on the way to admire a poster display announcing *Her Last Chance* was coming to the Oxford Picture House. Whose last chance of what he asked the doorman, who confirmed the hour.

– The telegram was taken at face value. It shouldn't have been. What if it wasn't Fanny but her husband who sent it?

– That would introduce premeditation.

– Motive, too.

– He could have sent it before they went dancing.

– Changes everything, wouldn't you say?

– No. It's only speculation.

– When did he book the Albemarle?

– There's no record of that.

Apart from the maid, now living in sheltered accommodation on Borstall

Hill, I have found nobody in Whitstable who remembers the extraordinary events of that spring night in the early nineteen twenties. The stopover which Thomas, fleeing London, was forced to take at the very same hotel to which his wife had earlier sent a telegram – an unlikely coincidence which should have received more attention – has faded from the memory of the town, along with the public disorder outside the Duke, the arrests, the subsequent trials, and the front page revelations in their wake.

I am beginning to wonder if I can make the story stand up.

Heart drumming, Thomas looks down at his rent spouse. There is a rush and tussle of words in his head, a clamour by each to be the last that she will ever hear.

He touches Fanny's cheek and whispers

– Parlee. Batter. Bleede.

He fingers the spurt on his jacket.

– Parlee, batter, bleede and dye.

The young woman seated in front of me whispers to her boyfriend.

– Donne, that's John Donne.

– Zit? Never seen 'im in anything before.

– Its poetry, airhead.

The script conference will argue about these lines for hours.

Who could have foreseen this? Here the danger, here the death, here.

Thomas places the knife beside the book on the sidetable.

A rosy bead of blood soils the upper board. Red coral blooms in the Aegean.

A crony of Tom's, somebody who is never identified by the police, will dispose of the blade later tonight.

The weapon remains undiscovered to this day, corroding in the toxic sludge of a canal in Camden, a covert toss from a quiet bridge on Gloucester Avenue.

I am not at liberty to tell you how I know this.

There is silence in the sitting room. Thomas is hurrying towards the bedroom to change his bloodied clothes. Halfway to the door something, a gurgle, perhaps imagined, a gasp post mortem, makes him turn his head back towards his wife. He blunders into a chair, toppling it to the floor.

And that's me, disturbed by the sudden clatter, thumping on the wall again as the opening scene of this domestic tragedy comes to an end. The last shot is a leisurely iris tightening around the knife, studio claret belling at its tip.

Cut to a shaky intertitle, as the tone of the piano brightens.

FLEEING THE SCENE

Thomas packs a suitcase. The cameraman undercranks the film at 17 frames per second, a speed which converts panic to comedy. The director underscores the switch with rippling arpeggios. Drawers and cupboard doors thrust open and retract like tappets in a top-notch combustion engine crafted by Ricardo. Tottering Thomas races and teeters around an accelerating bedroom.

A flannel dabs at a bloodstain then into the suitcase go: the greek blue, three other books, a bottle of spirits, documents, and socks. The gin is retrieved and swathed in tissue. A bottle of spirits, notebooks, a selection of pens wrapped in blotting paper, a scarf, a correlative, a truss, a spare shirt. Thomas takes back the scarf and puts it on, darts to the mirror, pouts, then tosses the scarf to the floor. He places a flower in a pot on the peak of the mound in the case. Bloom and stem are crushed beneath the lid. Tom sits on the case to close it. He's thrown off by the bounce of the bed. A second time too. At the third squash the clasp still refuses to catch. Aaaargh! Thomas puts his hands on his hips. He glares at the case. He scratches his head. The lid lowers itself slowly then springs back up defiantly. Tom gapes in stage surprise then masks his mouth with a hand. His expression becomes more serious. He picks out a sock. He holds the sock up to a window, studying the toe. A single thread dangles from the seam. He bites it and tosses the sock back into the case. The lid snaps shut. Tom jumps.

The audience stops laughing as the rhythm slows and Thomas returns to the sitting room. He looks towards the daybed.

In the foreground a dangling stockinged foot. Below it a shoe lying on its side.

Then, loud, a knock at the door. The eyes of Thomas balloon with alarm.

He was not suited to the role of murderer.

– All I wanted was a fling. Fanny became the way to burn my bridges, my excuse not to go back to America. I would stay and become a successful writer, another Henry James, but with better shaved prose. Instead I became a Paolo, paying medical bills, hellish bills for a woman who was no Francesca. Till death us do part was turning out to be an eternity. One moment alone it was that overcame us.

– We were good companions, Tom.

– You weren't company. You weren't solitude. You were my greatest mistake.

Letting himself in to the apartment three hours later, Tom's accomplice will see the sprawled body of a woman on a chaise longue, a smear on the wall, a knife on a table, and an overturned chair.

An artist of some standing, not one to miss the opportunity, Otto sketches the scene on stationery taken from Tom's desk. The foreshortening of the corpse is tricky. Mountainous feet, stringbean arms, an hourglass torso – the false starts multiply. He makes several attempts. Fanny is stretchered in blue pencil on cream bond for nearly an hour before the clean-up begins.

Otto stipples the curtains, stabbing at the paper, dap dap dap, with a blunted tip.

The knocking at the door continues, in beats of three, dap dap dap, while Thomas stands stock still in the tableau over my fireplace.

I turn away from the computer screen to compare the crime scene next door to the painting that hangs on my wall. I list the similarities and fret once again over the differences in an exercise I have completed many times before.

Yes, there is a gramophone in the room beyond the wall, on the cinema screen as on the canvas. But Thomas is not looking into its horn. What might he discover there if he did? In the painting Tom's coat is draped over a chair that is back on its feet. His hat is upon it. His bag is packed. Behind him a sprawled woman bleeds on a daybed. Many aspects of the crime are represented correctly. But someone has stripped the clothes from Fanny. The rug has gone. The door to the apartment has been removed. Why? What is the painter trying to tell us? Was the first detective to enter the apartment really carrying a club? Was the second clutching a net? Of course not, they never do, except in metaphors and movies, dubious yarns or surreal daubs. Nor could there have been three witnesses watching at the window, hovering twenty feet above the street. A probable fourth is faceless, hidden by Tom's shoulder. All six men are wearing powder and lipstick. Are the cosmetics for a film shoot? Lazily, in my opinion – but it may be a ploy – the artist has rough-painted mountains behind the gawkers, dodging the labour-intensive rendition of the redbrick façade and iron balconies of the neighbouring block.

I knock. An artist nicks. Thomas pulls a deep breath.

When he opens the door there are no detectives poised to arrest him. Just an aggrieved neighbour unable to contain his anger.

– I really must protest.

– Not at all, it's me that should apologise.

– Tom this is getting beyond a

– Fanny and I are sorry about the racket. Very sorry. You won't be disturbed again.

– You said the same thing yesterday.

– We realise our, um, exchanges cause a disturbance. That our conduct as tenants has verged, at times, on the unacceptable. It really will not happen again.

– The commotion has to stop.

– The dispute between Fanny and myself, our differences of opinion, have now come to an end. I can assure you of that.

– They better had Tom. It's like you're in the room with us.

– I do understand. My wife is on her way to Tunbridge Wells for a week or so. Believe me, you will be troubled no more.

On the daybed, obscured by the door, Fanny bleeds heavily. Lancashire sap sunsets into a pair of silk cushions handsewn by her mother.

Tom's wife joins him at the door. She curves round her husband with a lop-sided smile.

– Hey, join us fradrink, why don't you?

– Mrs Stern. Good evening.

– This way to the party, pal.

– Another time thank you. It's been a long day. We're a little tired. Thin walls and well, you know. I'll say goodnight to you both.

The neighbour returns to his room where the accusatory painting shines like a warning notice under a spotlight. Magritte's The Murderer Menaced, an aftershock registered in Paris five years later, bears witness to Tom's crime in situ. Sergeant Winchell will seize the canvas next week.

– The painting is circumstantial evidence, sir. As you can see, the floorboards in the image are misaligned. We will be lifting them today. The shadow of the chair points to the murderer. The image is inconclusive,

I do grant you that, but it is central to the investigation. The painting will be returned, I will see to it, when the trial is over.

– But my insurance won't cover that.

– No sir, I don't suppose it does.

Back at my desk, I hear the door to the apartment close. There are footsteps on the landing, more steps descending the stairs. Thomas is going out. The stairwell funnels the boom of the street door upwards until, shuddering and spent, it falls in the porch of Fanny's ear. She doesn't hear it. Hurrying south towards the Marylebone Road, Thomas slides between buttered cones of light draped around the streetlamps by Grammatte. Otto transforms them into petalled shellbursts on black stalks. Then Thomas is gone, formless into the painterly murk of the evening.

– No drum fatalistic? No geranium?

– I don't understand.

The detective should be highly intelligent but not superhuman.

– Answer the sergeant.

– Drum? Geranium?

– As I said, I don't understand. But no. I don't think so. Neither.

– What the killer fails to do may be as significant as what he does. Do you agree?

– Why am I here?

Two days later an Abraham from Whitechapel, a swaggering infantryman who made it through Ypres, says a man fitting Thomas's description flagged down his cab at roughly seven o'clock that evening.

The distributors wanted subtitles for this scene. It opens with a shot of an avuncular sergeant standing under a flickering blue lamp. The interview takes place at a police station on the Harrow Road, a tram hop from the Coliseum where I view it.

– Victoria, the station please, this goyisher feller says to me. I am in an immense hurry driver. I've a train at ten to the hour. That's what the guiser is saying, all of it, totes. Not a dicky narry a fegaleh more for the whole of the run. We done?

I stand as two latecomers crab towards a pair of empty seats.

– What more can I tell you? So not so much. He is a scribbler. Pencil and papiere on his handkoffer.

– Handcuffs?

– Handkoffer. The suitcase. Complaining at the bumpings and the brakings. You want me to be stopped I think. I do not say this, not with the hurry he's in. No, he did not state his vinyl destination. You are knowing yours? Anyting else? I'm happy to help zee politsey but I have to be working for a living.

His palms stay closed as his eyebrows rise. More questions follow.

The cab, a Unic, rasps past Marble Arch, startling the last nags hauling hansoms through the fogbound past. The vehicle grinds its way along Park Lane.

– I tellt him no need for panic sir, veal be there in time for the last zug down. He is khalere, know what I mean, a worrier, thinks he will miss the ban. In Grosvenor Place he sayed pullover. I pullover. Out he gets and puts his shraybing through the door. He was short onder fare at Victoria. Vay. He is making the apologies. That's not it I says, that's not it. I can't pay the rent with your sorries. He gibs me a timepiece and kart it says Crippence Court Gardens. I knock the door and here we go. Thinked I could trust him but a goy, well how can you tell? No disrespect you understand?

No, he didn't ask if there was a reward.

That pause in Grosvenor Square wasn't followed up by the police. In the hastily scrawled message, which I have located in a private collection in Germany, Thomas appealed for help to Wilhelm Otto Dix, the highly decorated former staff sergeant – Iron Cross, second class – of a Boche machine gun unit. The muzzle-boosted Maxims under Dix's command had shredded hundreds of our Tommies in the recent war.

Curiously, there is no record of Herr Dix visiting London at the time. The note appeals to him to go to the apartment in the mansion block immediately and to tidy up 'anything untoward' that he finds there. An explanation will follow.

– I find that in order to escape trouble I shall be obliged to absent myself for a time. I will be eternally grateful, Otto, mein Schatz, if you could do me this service. Mit viele Liebe, Tom.

To this day I still don't understand how the Flanders veterhun was able to get in and out of the apartment without being seen. Otto disposed of the soiled clothing and the cushions, cleansed the trail of cherries from the rug and dragged a cupboard in front of the gore-streaked wall. By means unknown he conveyed Fanny's body two and a half miles north to a vacant property in Hilldrop Crescent in Camden. Not a single resident of the block, nor anyone living in the one opposite, saw hide nor hair of of Herr Dix.

– Erase the traces.

– Easier said than done.

Years later, looking back, Winchell recalled his frustration.

– I was trying to get the hang of a case which was becoming more difficult at every turn. You don't jump to the conclusion that murder has been committed merely because a wife has disappeared and a husband has told lies about it. My quarry had gone, but the manner of his going pointed to guilt.

Otto Dix confessed to his involvement in the late sixties, in a diary entry made just before his death. The account mentions drawings he made at the time and a painting, a London Lustmord. His widow burned the journal but she was able to recall a few details when I located her in northern Germany.

– It was only a paragraph. Otto wrote that he had once disposed of a body and a weapon for a friend in England. Whether this really happened, I don't know.

– You doubt it?

– My husband was confused towards the end. He was between two strokes. His memories were contaminated with stories that he had heard, with anxieties and with gossip and dreams, and with the fanciful interpretations that critics had begun to force on his paintings.

What else did the entry say?

– He said that he had made drawings on the spot, in the building where the woman was killed and in the room to which he moved her. It wasn't clear to me when the killing happened or who had done it, if it had occurred at all. The poor woman.

– Did you ever see the drawings?

– They are well known. He gave me a watercolour based on them in the summer of 1922, a few months after we married. A woman with her clothing torn away and her throat cut. She was tangled in a blanket and sprawled on her back on bare boards by a bed. Her bumbel gaped at the centre of the scene. My husband and I were not squeamish people you know. 'I must experience all of life's abysses for myself,' that's what he used to say. There was much chaos in him. We placed a lustmord above our dining table in Berlin. When friends came round for dinner some of them – the weaker kind – lost their appetite.

As Martha speaks the black feathers on her mourning hat shiver. Dark sequins in the veil suspended from its brim scuttle like insects across her face. The bugs throw no shadows as they circle the tight red lips stapled to her whitewash frown.

– We cannot be without veils in this life.

– Tom will take the veil, or whatever monks do.

Dix dumps the body in a top floor room without a view. He makes the scene look like one of the sex murders given front-page treatment back home in Germany. He has a collection of these lurid cuttings on his studio wall.

– So you want me to play dead, you naughty boy?

– Bitte sprechen Sie nicht.

– Otto, dearest. Tom was never this much fun.

Corpse on the mattress, head hanging down towards the floor. Corpse on the floor, one foot up on the mattress. A toppled chair, a bloodied sheet. No sheet, a wine bottle, no wine bottle. Otto arranges the scene to his liking. He takes his time. He sketches Fanny, tattooed and sprawled by a proxy deathbed. Without telling Thomas, he makes a painting from these drawings when he returns to Dresden. In the studio he collages souvenirs from London on to its surface. He gives the dead tart's boudoir a mischievous view — Crippence Court Gardens at night. A light burns in just one window, the home of the Sterns. Dix's dealer, Nierendorf, takes the finished work. He sells it on quickly.

For sixteen years the evidence of Tom's crime hangs in plain sight on a drawing room wall in the Konigsallee in Dusseldorf. In 1938, in June, it is handed over to Gestapo director Heinrich Muller in exchange for the owner's safe passage to Paris.

Muller scrawled a charcoal note on the back of the frame. It's still there.

Received from the Jew Ottstein for

A SEAT ON THE LAST TRAIN

The cab draws up on the forecourt at Victoria Station at 7.30pm, dropping Thomas at the entrance to the left of the two termini. He waves a grasping porter away.

Nine decades later, working the cold case, I reconstruct his flight.

I will recapitulate the incidents of those days in as exact a manner as possible. They were elicited subsequently at the trial by a process of long and tedious cross-examinations.

As Thomas argues with the driver, I stow the book I have been skimming – *The Mysterious Affair at Styles* – in my back pack. It's by Agatha Christie, a new chick on the block in the Sherlock game.

I watch the altercations between passenger, porter and driver, an agitated mumming too far off for me to hear, as I launch a camera to record my target's approach.

Thomas gives the driver a card and his wristwatch. He twosteps through the horse turds and hurries past the pollards begging beneath the arch.

– Tuppence for a veteran, sir?

A gauntlet of paperboys chants headlines. A blind girl sits on a nearby step.

– Chaplin in London! Railmen 'tensify mining crisis! Last troops leave Curragh! Sisters dead in opium den!

– Flower, sir?

Thomas enters a smoke-shrouded chaos: coal porters, luggage porters, rough sleepers, horses and distressed livestock, automated announcements, mailsacks, uniformed staff, sushi bars, label stickers, Southern Rail apologists, queuebusters with wifi dispensers, fruit sellers, trolley pushers, commuters, milk cans, Chinese tourists, commercial travellers, an Italian crocodile, clover kickers up to haggle mortgages, womankind with hatboxes, rent boys in designer swag, parasols and bonnets, police officers in stab vests with strap-on semiautomatics, infantrymen slouched by carbine stooks.

I prefer the shadow of a train, passing over a face, to a whole railway station.

– March on Rome. Waterin' of milk must end! Shameless Doctor Stopes.

Tom visits a window in the booking office. He posts cash and pockets a ticket.

– Departs in fifteen minutes, platform four sir. Thataway.

Striding across the concourse, herded through smoulder and steam by whistles, barks and the bustle of porters, Thomas is acutely aware of the reality of sin.

– I pushed her over. And the result? I am afraid of all that has happened, and of all that is to come.

In the Hollywood flick his words were distorted way past recognition.

– Well, I guess I've done murder… I'll think about it tomorrow.

Tom won't be apprehended tonight. Back in the mansion block his neighbours enjoy an unusually tranquil evening. Fanny is notoriously unpredictable, so she won't be missed for a number of days. There's no blood soaking through the ceiling into the flat below. The help isn't due until Monday. And as soon as staff sergeant Dix picks up the message he will do his duty.

– Another bottle before you go, Otto?

– Danke, the night is jung. Prost!

– When we walk past work, dearie, would you mind if I pop upstairs to feed the cat? I've set some scraps aside. They do neglect it so, poor thing.

– I'll knock on Fanny's door, I think. Just to check she's all right.

To the commuters draining from the city centre to sofas in the suburbs, the identity of the gaunt figure making his way towards platform four, his motives, his next move and the condition of his soul are all a matter of indifference.

The telltale painting by Dix will not be exhibited for another three years, and then only in enemy territory, northern Germany. Fanny's family, Thomas's bank colleagues and literary set, the neighbours and the investigating officers are all unlikely to see it. And it will be a further three years before the secondary canvas, painted by Magritte, develops a back story.

It's far too soon for hue and cry, for the chase and the capture, for the learned urging of noose and stake and flames. But they will follow.

As he approaches the gate, Thomas passes a portly sergeant, a stolid bobby striped for years of service. A walrus curtain hangs below his ruddy nose.

Sergeant Winchell, moist with malt, has been ordered to Victoria by his great uncle, the police commissioner. He is there to prevent Bolsheviks and other troublemakers reaching Chislet, Snowdown and Tilmanstone, unruly villages in the Kent coalfields, northern infestations of the Garden.

– These Red agitators will subvert the union, William. They will ruin the industry, the Empire and the country. They are turning their bellows on a strike against wage reductions and if we let them they will stoke it into a bloody revolution. They're mostly from the north. Bankrolled by the Jews and Moscow. Find them. Drag them in. They must not pass. Catch these weevils Winchell. Scotch their evil before it spreads.

I will follow that order to the letter, Winchell thinks. I'll have two quick fingers in the tavern before I leave. He fumbles the ear cone on to the hook of the candlestick phone. Ten minutes later he is briefing his men.

– The Reds can have Georgia, wherever that is, but we're not going to let them sink Bolshevik fangs into Kent. Question anybody who looks or sounds out of place. Bring 'em back here if they can't account for their journey. That includes everyone carrying the *Herald*.

A gent topped with a dome, tipped in grey spats, will be above suspicion tonight.

Tom's getaway does not rely on an elaborate or incredible disguise. His improvised escape plan draws on the advice of a critic hooked on gumshoe. His chances depend on his own counsel.

Whiskery, whiskied Winchell, station sergeant sot, doesn't turn his head as the dapper banker halts to have his ticket nipped.

Neither does he see me following behind.

Our meetings will take place tomorrow.

In an hour's time Marie Lloyd, the suckbottle Queen of the Music Hall, will stumble on to the stage of the Palace Theatre opposite the station. The sergeant will join fifteen hundred beery voices for the chorus, just as Thomas has before him.

the guards and the porters
came rahnd by the score
she told 'em all she'd never 'ad
'er ticket punched before

Winchell is entitled to an off duty singalong but he is going to regret it. In the morning he will be roused for a manhunt, shortly after a murder is discovered in the apartment directly beneath his own.

A small world, held together by coincidences. That's what the genre insists on.

As I approach the ticket barrier, taxi drivers and chauffeurs are holding up handwritten notices. It's a common sight at major railway stations.

All of the placards say the same thing.

HOT PURSUIT

I nod to the waiting drivers as I pass. They cheer and wave back. One offers a fist bump.

– Goowan, goo get the Jodrell.

A gaffer leaps down from a second class carriage. He weaves a foxtrot through the arrivals and dragalongs, dancing with a holdall held high above his head. As he passes through the gate, Charlie Roscuro scans the row of waiting wheelmen. He points at the furthest. The driver frowns then folds and pockets his sign. He takes the bag from the lighting engineer and leads his fare towards a side exit.

– Crippence Court Gardens, close to Regents Park. Quick as you can.

– Your wish is my starting pistol. Car's this way twinkletoes.

I slip through the press at the gate. Rising on my stubs, I can't tell which of the flotilla of domes bobbling forard caps our Tom.

There are new and strange objects in the foreground, to be drawn accurately in proportion to the more familiar ones which now approach the horizon, where all but the most eminent become invisible to the naked eye.

Waddlers with wheelies block my path and slow me down. I squeeze past towers of cheese. Moms and pops and sprogs and gramps bottleneck the platform. Bales of cloth narrow my path. A man milks a cow into a small jug. Somewhere a kettle is about to boil.

I won't lose Tom. I already know where he's going. I bought my ticket ten minutes before his arrival, certain that he would make his way to the Albemarle Hotel in Cliftonville, a refuge high above the English Channel. It's the kind of spot where credulous people kid themselves they can see France. An airy and well to do resort, it's somewhere Tom has played possum before.

– So whither I go ye know, and the way ye know.

– Deffo. I'll be sticking to you like treacle.

Last November I looked on as Tom and Fanny sipped tea in the ornamental gardens on the clifftop. Earlier that day they had dispatched his mother stateside on a steamer. Until that visit, he'd not seen mum for six years. Fanny had caused a scene. He was relieved to wave goodbye. He strummed a banjoline and cracked jokes as I loitered beneath their window. I sat by the bandstand on Fort Green, waiting for him to emerge.

As veterans marched on the cenotaph, waving pawn tickets in the air, I tailed Tom to a Margate beach shelter at the far end of the tram line. He had sat alone with a newspaper and a book that he didn't open. He had looked on as a motorised lifeboat raced towards a tragedy and returned empty-handed. It was a time of drought. At midday he had paddled in the surf, the bottoms of his pants rolled. For lunch he bought dried peach from a higgler's basket. It was only a few months ago. It was ninety years ago. I think Tom is hoping to retrieve the peace he felt last year.

He won't manage that tonight. I know. I've got the affliction. I foresuffer it all.

There he is, mounting the steps into first class. The villain climbs into the saddle of an iron horse, ready to ride from town.

I must try and get a seat nearby, a sightline at least, in earshot if possible.

That was easy. Tom and I are sitting opposite each other. We are sharing a table with two commuters travelling back to Kent. Cropheads with specs and non-iron shirts. We sit in a strew of coffee beakers, pungent snacks, backpacks, beercans and mobile phones. Headphone leads snake beneath freesheets. Project managers phone ahead for pick-ups, family reports and takeaways.

A pageant of silent screens serves soap and sporting highlights – kisses, catches, blows — to stragglers aisling for arsespace.

Thomas gets out a notebook and pencil. He jots and pauses then he jots some more.

I saw on the opposing platform
Clerks shaking alien spears
On death's stage
A clerk shakes his umbrella
Yooble a spear sacrifice

A distant whistle shrills. The captive pea sings.

The train departs with a series of jolts, unpredictable, that rock us in our seats.

On the table before me, a few inches from his own, the hand of the one who will betray him.

Honneger. Schaeffer. Chemin de fer. Honneger, Schaeffer, chemindefer.

Honneger, Schaeffer, chemindefer. Honnegerschaefferchemindefer. Chemindefer. Chemindefer. De fer. De fer. De fer. De fer fare fare.

The rattle of wheels and the rhythm of prose are essential complements.

The shudder smoothes to rhythmic judder. We glance down the dark trough of the Thames. We scale the chimneys of the power station. We take in the view from the gasholders. We peer into the shadowed park.

Passive watching from a seat in a train is a precursor of the cinema.

The audience relaxes to tracking shots of terraces and factories.

– What's next?

– More of the same. Library shots.

– There's too much daylight. Crunch the luminescence.

In Crippence Court Gardens Otto drags a cupboard in front of the bloodied wall.

It is not until the 1960s that Thomas and I come across the sketches that he has made of the crime scene, those he will soon make of the dumping ground, and the spectacular canvas he will paint of Fanny as a murdered prostitute.

Tom will see reproductions of his co-conspirator's work in a catalogue raissoné in the London Library. From that moment he fears his days are numbered.

– I had been accepted into the church. I was an editor with influence and resources. A household name. The stage had welcomed me. I was a husband once again, and properly so. President of the library. Was it going to end like this?

– Maybe. Those who stand proud have no sure footing.

His lawyer knew the score from the start of the hearing.

– Painters, sculptors, indeed the postwar visual arts in general, these were always a blind spot for my client. He simply didn't pay enough attention to painting as one aspect, one constellation, of time past that might speak to time present. I'm sorry to say that's what led to his downfall.

When he comes across the images of Fanny, Thomas blanches. He slams the doorstop volume shut, shunting his seat backwards over the polished wooden floor. The screech of the chair persists, even when it rocks. As the legs prod at the boards Tom flips a backward somersault through the air. He makes a perfect landing, no sway or steadying step. Then he droops and palms his face.

The eminent readers sharing the table are startled. At the subsequent trial, one of the country's leading mystery writers testified to Tom's out-of-character behaviour.

– I was not present at the moment of the crime. I have no tangible evidence. I do not know the man in the dock personally. All I am sure of is that the behaviour I witnessed suggests a preoccupation with guilt.

Her hands shake as she speaks. She tickles invisible ivories that only she can hear.

As for me, I stumbled across London Lustmord (1922, oil on canvas and collage, 165cm x 135cm) in a Mayfair gallery on Davies Street. I recognised the drawn features and embedded beads of my missing neighbour straight away, along with the actual bracelet, entrenched in the paint, that had once chipped at Tom's glasses. A price list from Hephaistos pasted to the foreground was the final confirmation.

I purchased the canvas with a loan and stored it in an old warehouse by the harbour in Whitstable. I knew it was evidence of something but I wasn't sure what. From that moment onwards, I felt compelled to investigate the murder registered by the canvas, whatever the cost to my reputation, my relationships and my career. Little did I know then where this headstrong impulse would take me.

Otto furls the rug, securing his Fanny roll with twine.

Our train races through a storm. Its steam whistle bagpipes like a screech owl over beating drums as the carriage in which we sit flashes across the painted metal screen of the Oxford Street Picture House in Whitstable.

A SNOWMAN BLEW HIM AWAY

As we reach Bromley South, Thomas is writing in his journal.

– I had no horror of my action. I only felt the repetition of it, over and over.

Then he rests. His flaps stay down until brakes scream Gravesend.

Fingers of moist smoke rise through the iron fence above the railway cutting, reaching for a governess and a young girl. The woman has a book and a puppy in her lap. Her eyes are turned on the artist. The child looks down on the Gare Saint Lazare. Cattle graze a valley straddled by the Belah viaduct. A father dozes in first class, abandoning his daughter to the attentions of a young suitor. An engine emerges from behind a tree, toylike and diminutive in the Delaware gap, puffing scrawl below monumental clouds. On the plains, by ruptured track, Cheyenne warriors lay in wait for the iron horse. Subdued, they take to snowy heights and shun the line. Fumes petal into the angular roof of the Gare St Lazare. A popular station. A hare bolts over the bridge at Maidenhead, a locomotive in pursuit. Leafless birch trees are dusted with soot as peasant women forage grimy herbs. An engine cools in dwell time between the trees in Arles. A white horse watches from a scalped down, as seen from carriage number three. A distant train quits the roofscape, leaving behind a city of arches and fruit. An engine emerges from an empty fireplace. It terminates at Polish gates, then rusts in jungle. Twins sit in facing seats. One reads, one sleeps. In each of their laps there is a black hat with a red feather. One has fruit, one has flowers, one has lost her blue gloves.

– Une bousculade de détails. Only film can do this.

The director asserts his authority by talking nonsense. The editor and the intern ignore him. Later that night they text each other.

– Bit of a tosser I thought.

– Only film can do this!

The platform of an observation carriage clanks as it is dragged through Mexico towards Los Angeles. A bride and her husband admire the view. It is the evening of their wedding day. She will recall his words.

– We could put an end to this misery if you'd just jump.

If there was ever a Jekyll and Hyde, it was Mr Charlie Chaplin.

Bellisima locomotiva! Going right on the end of the line.

Three miles ahead of us, a hackneyed villain with a moustache is tying a gagged woman to moonlit track by a crossing near Fawkham station.

One mile behind our train, in hot pursuit and closing, four cops pump a handcart. A sergeant yells go faster at them, faster.

From the window of our carriage I spot a car with celebrity racing driver Barney Oldfield illuminated at the wheel. It passes at high speed.

The victim's eyes widen with stage fear. The car dustclouds to a halt. The train is nearing. There is a struggle. The villain is cast into the dust. Freed, the heroine throws her arms around her rescuer. The reunited couple are backlit by the headlamps of the car.

Tying a woman to the tracks as a locomotive approaches is one of the earliest set pieces of the cinema. It was stolen from the stage. Not much turns out to be new.

Mabel and Barney break their clinch to wave as our train passes.

Before she became Chaplin's co-writer and leading lady, Mabel Normand was clad in chains and lashed to the rails in Barney Oldfield's *Race for a Life*, a comedy chase directed by Mack Sennett .

Thomas saw the film in its first week of release. As we kettle through rural Kent his eyes close to recall those of Mabel Sweet and Lovely.

– Eyes he dare not meet in dreams?

– Why not.

– Eyes that last he saw in tears? That he will see no more?

– Take your pick.

As we pass Sole Street, twenty seven miles out from Victoria, the Los Angeles Police Department is questioning Normand about the murder of her lover, the director William Desmond Taylor. The shooting has been linked to the Hollywood cocaine trade. The star wears an off the shoulder pipe of silk, with precious stones and stilettos.

– Talk, lady. This ain't no silent movie.

– I blew Bill a kiss then a snowman blew him away.

A girl and a train, a girl and a gun, the history of film. Off the screen, homicide by Bradshaw – using a locomotive rather than the bound timetable – is a risky method of killing. The victim has to be conveyed to a remote spot where there is access to the track. Although photogenic, heavy chains are a cumbersome, unreliable form of restraint. To peg the victim to the ground a mallet is needed. Almost always, an assistant is required. In Sennett's case he also had to steal the train. The risk of interruption is considerable. The wrap will be delayed by signal problems, mechanical failures, planned engineering works, leaves on the line and loco engineers on leave. Replacement buses, strikes, bank holiday timetables and staff pulling sickies derail the best laid plans. Sergeant Winchell says that no one determined to inflict defunctitude would adopt such a hazardous procedure.

The body of an unidentified woman in her twenties was found on the rails near the village of Durali in August 2014, according to a report in the *Hindustan Times*. The investigation revealed that the victim was tied to the track with three dupattas. Her mouth had been stuffed with cloth. A train had passed over the helpless victim, cutting her body into two.

Glass shelving above my head, perforations and strip lighting above that. A male likeness changing a baby's nappy. A man and a woman waiting beside an arrow. A seated figure with a child on its lap. One with a cane, another with a dog. A swelling gravida. An exclamation mark on a bell. A blue triangle boxing a capital P. The need for this seat may not be immediately obvious.

I nod off briefly. When I wake the lights of steamers and gunboats ribbon the soak at Rochester. Thomas is reading my Christie.

I want to keep an open mind about him but it's hard to forget the character reference that Virginia gave in court.

– Sordid, emotional, intense. A kind of Crippen, in a mask.

Tom notices my waking. He reads aloud across the table.

– The dead woman had not the gift of commanding love. Her death was a shock and a distress, but she would not be passionately regretted. You marked these lines. Why this passage, precisely?

He's sharp. Direct. Not as aloof as I'd been told to expect.

I cannot read his expression. I'm not even sure what to look for. He's on the run. He may be in shock. Has he realised what I'm up to? Is there a chance he'll attack me? I will not fight with him on the roof of a moving train. If that's what the audience wants, they've picked the wrong show.

He hands the book back to me.

– I hope you don't mind. I read any detective story with enjoyment.

– Hang on to it.

– Are you sure?

– My address is in the front. Post it back when you're done.

– I couldn't.

– I've taken all I want from it.

– In that case I will.

A close quarters pursuit is not without risks, I explained to the jury. My mobile phone was down, the signal gone. I was unable to notify anyone of my movements. It was possible I was being lured to a remote spot in Kent. I might meet my end at the hands of a ruthless editor. Even more foolishly, I had given the accused my address. What was I thinking? He could track me down to enforce my silence. Had the table turned? I feared so.

Thomas closes his eyes again. He's no pin up, that's for sure. His mouth gapes like the Medway. It silts like the Swale. The carious ruins of Rochester castle lean from his gums.

– Surely, of all futile occupations, this cataloguing of features is the worst?

Virginia will keep sticking her oar in. I must find something to shut her up.

– Landscape is a passive creature which lends itself to an author's mood.

Am I in danger? I didn't think so, not now ninety years later, not then chemin deferring in the dark, nor here in row D seat 5. I'm safe at my keyboard lodged in the one and ninepennies, steaming through Chatham. I become less anxious after his burial in 1965.

– Of all the machines that have throbbed their way across the kinema screen none is more potent, none has moved to a finer measure, than the railway engine on the track. Directors today don't give a damn what Legerne wrote in 1925. They watch their rivals. They shoot without a rear view mirror. They aren't readers anymore. The movie camera and the motor car, flight and film, they took longer to click. Car chases thrill the boys, unzipping their fears. Airliners are airborne drawing rooms, immobile. Film and track are tongue and groove, a tight fit, mapping each other's motion.

At the end of my talk, nobody has a question. The chair steps in.

– Before digital, did people talk more on trains?

– I don't think so. We read newspapers.

Not on one journey, north to Oban.

– I'll start. An easy one. *L'Arrivée d'un train en gare de La Ciotat.*

– 1896. *The Great Train Robbery.*

– 1903. *The Iron Horse.*

– 1924. *The General.*

– Before 1930. I'm not sure. 28?

– 1927. That's one to me. *Shanghai Express*!

– 32. *The Lady Vanishes*. Please don't.

– 1938.

– *North by Northwest* for a bonus?

– 1959.

– Wow, you know your stuff. Two up to you.

– *Pacific 321.*

– Pass, don't know it.

– A must see. Mitry, 1949. *Murder on the Orient Express.*

– I was in flares. Early seventies. 73?

– Four. I'm three ahead.

– *The American Friend.*

– The what?

– Premieres next month. Wenders.

– That's not fair!

– The Polish one. *Night Train*. The best.

– Kawalerowicz. Brilliant. But it was 1959. You're out of sequence.

– Damn. You won.

– We forgot *Brief Encounter*.

– I won't say goodbye if you don't.

We were together for five years. She's married to the director of the British Film Archive now. They've got kids, two boys, and horses.

How did Tom know Otto? When did they meet and where? It wasn't when Tom was in Munich, in 1911. Dix was in Dresden then, studying at the School of Arts and Crafts. There is one moment, a possible crossing of paths in 1914, when the clandestine alliance of the American from St Louis and the patriot from Untermhaus may have been forged. When the Kaiser declared war Tom was a student in Marburg. It was fourteen days before he slipped away to France by train, passing through Frankfurt and Cologne. Dix disappeared from view at the very same time. His whereabouts during those tense days of troop movements, timetable disruptions and general confusion, is uncertain. He had slipped supervision. Marburg was the opportunity. In the letters which have survived Tom is reticent about his movements and contacts. Was it here, in a gothic bierkeller below the schloss, far from the eyes of modern scholarship, that the lethal partnership was contracted?

– Language, thought and feeling have been sundered, Otto. The philosophies of east and west are rent. I will reunite them.

– I'm going to resurrect sixteenth-century painting for our time.

– Poetry and sensibility must be restored. New verse with ancient rhyme.

– The example of the masters. Expression and precision.

– We will master the alchemies of myth, sex, the city, philosophy!

– Painting is the effort to produce order; order in yourself.

– Poetry too. Impersonality will be my touchstone.

– Sachlichheit will be mine.

– This war will not divide us.

– We shall assist each other.

– This is our treaty.

– Our pact.

They wash down the oath with schnapps. They search for a dancehall.

– Stern lived in Germany, sarge. On two occasions, in Munich and in Marburg. He is a resident alien and he has Boche associates, including a ranking hun officer.

Winchell candlesticks the commissioner that afternoon. His right ear flattens beneath the cone. The mouthpiece tents his tash.

– We've also questioned the neighbours, sir. Stern confided to one that he had considered returning to Germany during the war, to teach in a university as a so-called neutral. Hell's name what's neutral in that? In his apartment there are letters from German correspondents, along with records of financial transactions, some of them involving many thousands of pounds. There are notes and letters in many languages. I have removed them all for closer analysis. It's my view, sir, that we should no longer consider the Crippence Court case to be a crime of passion. There is something impersonal, cosmopolitan, and possibly arthouse about this killing.

The train draggles through the moonlit emptiness of Kent.

Nearly two thousand miles away, in Leningrad, armed commissars are patrolling the corridors of the Rimsky-Korsakov State Conservatory. Not yet silenced by Stalin, the composer Vladimir Deshevov mounts the footplate of a grand express piano. He launches into Rails, Opus 16, a futuristic composition for the industrial proletariat. Its accelerating trundle carries us into the night.

The bright interior of the carriage, emptier now we have crossed the Medway, is reflected in the windows. Raindrops beetle across the glass. The train is flanked with static projections of itself. I peel the layers of imagery apart, trying to locate the landscape. In the distance wooded hills hunch hedgehog backs at pylons. At seventy seconds the piece by Deshevov ends abruptly. As the overtones ebb, an intertitle looms and leaves as if it is the nameboard for a station where we're not going to stop.

NOTHING TO SEE OUT HERE

Scowling and shaking his head, the lighting engineer unfolds and refolds the telegram a third time, then a fourth.

Thomas departs 8pm away until Sat.

It is clear what Fanny expects but her words are guarded. The invitation isn't as direct as he first thought.

– Where the eff is she?

Roscuro makes his way back down the stairs of the mansion block. He's disappointed the grass widow isn't home for a roll in the hay.

As he issues from the arch he is stopped by a police officer.

– I'm sorry to trouble you sir. We've had reports. My sergeant's got some questions. Can you tell me if your wife is in?

Fifteen minutes later the landlord unlocks the door of the apartment. Two detectives stand by.

Does one have a club in his hand, and the other a net? I leave my desk and crack the door open to check.

– Go back inside sir please. There's nothing to see out here.

The morgue is cold. It smells of Lysol. The voice of the police surgeon clatters around the ceramic walls.

– Cats are not permitted in this building under any circumstances or at any time. Whenever someone dies, or when a cadaver is laid out for cutting or display, you must close every window and shut every door. If a moggie does get in, it starts with the face. The cheeks and the nostrils usually. Especially when it's not being fed.

– They neglect it so, poor thing.

The dead woman's face is unrecognisable. Her jewellery has been removed. The police were unable to say if this happened before the corpse was placed in the ambulance. At the time of the trial the whereabouts of Fanny's bracelets, rings and necklace were unknown. Most are still missing.

We have been delayed at Faversham, with no explanation, for fifteen minutes. At last there's a short blast from a whistle. Doors slam and we're moving again.

The surgeon stands by Fanny's corpse.

– I found this most curious. There are words tattooed on her navel, what's left of it. 'Cruel', that's clear enough, and something like 'reeding'. See here? 'Desire'. That's all I can make out until she's been untangled. There's more on her back, and some of it is German.

As our train passes between an engine shed and the shadowy maze of a Faversham brickyard, the guard skids the door to our booth open. He apologises for the interruption. They have just heard that railwaymen further along the coast have withdrawn their labour. The train will terminate at the next station.

– The strikers are supporting the miners sir. The pay dispute. I regret to inform you that Whitstable Town and Tankerton will be the last stop. Yes, yes, I do understand the problem. I will try to secure onward transportation on arrival.

The Triple Alliance was formed in 1914 by the Miners Federation of Great Britain, the National Union of Railwaymen and the National Transport Workers' Federation. The three unions are the prop legs of the labour movement, braced and muscular, with toes entrenched in every town.

Prime Minister Lloyd George is impressed.

– Gentlemen, you have fashioned in the Triple Alliance of unions represented by you a most powerful instrument. I feel bound to tell you that, in our opinion, we are at your mercy.

The old Welsh Goat That Won the War said that to a miners' leader who repeated it to a youthful Aneurin Bevan. Our end is himself. Lloyd George had more to say, as always.

– If a force arises in the state that is stronger than the state itself, it must be ready to take on the functions of the state, or withdraw and accept the authority of the state.

The wily, repetitive old goat.

– Hold on a minute. This is about pay!

– You are escalating the dispute, not us.

– This meeting is over, gentlemen.

– God help us unless the government wins.

The lost train pants in the dark saltmarsh, just short of Whitstable, waiting for a sign.

– Why aren't we moving?

– There's no one to operate the signal.

Thomas wipes his glasses and puts them back on. He sits patiently. He takes his glasses off. He wipes them again. He stretches his legs beneath the table. He wipes his spectacles once more, purely for the delay and the duration yielded by the wiping of his eyewear. He studies his reflection. He wipes his glasses again.

Against the tactics of speed, of noise, set tactics of slowness, of silence.

Are the delays deliberate? Are they part of a trap? Is a net closing around him?

In the delay between Tom and the coast, a human wall, a wall of massing miners and engine drivers, of brakemen and of signalmen. Stokers and dockers climb on to their shoulders, waving spades and hooks. Seamen stamp across the shingle bearing nets. Commissars lurk by the faceless barricade. Libraries and a cathedral smoulder in the mid distance. Constables are leaving unlit sheds in the reeds and creeping towards the train.

The police surgeon extracts a pencil stub from one of Fanny's wounds. It has a blue sleeve and a broken point. Sergeant Winchell strokes his moustache.

The medical examiner extracts slivers of oil paint, Dresden blue, from Fanny's midriff rips. Sergeant Winchell scratches his head.

– Keep your hands to yourself why can't you.

The surgeon resents being stroked and scratched by the sergeant. He will make an official complaint. Winchell will get an informal warning from his uncle.

If I have been reading, then sometimes my mind would be so strangely snatched away, and possessed with other things, that I have neither known, nor regarded, nor remembred so much as the sentence that but now I have read.

Thomas is looking at the ceiling of the carriage. What's he thinking?

How do you describe the thoughts of a man facing the rope?

In a trice he was on the trap-doors with his legs strapped together and a rope around his neck. One swift glance round to be assured that all was right, and my hand shot to the lever. Thud! The fatal doors fell. The slack rope tightened, and in an instant was still.

Tom rubs his throat. He sees me watching and looks away.

Behind bars on the carriage window, Bertie in Brixton. Three sides to every argument. Triangles, triple alliances, Germany, France, fractals, the miners. Fanny's gift of commanding love. So one as so threefold, are and is. Austria-Hungary, the father, the son, a trinity pilot. Paps was in bricks, never met the wife. Transport workers, sheep herders, wise dudes, cubes, the Holy Ghost. Parson's in the house. Will Lady Rothermere cough for the dosh? Three men in a boat. Don't let the nightsticks catch you. Fades and montages shimmer over the watching saltmarsh.

A touch of the hoo-has.

These are my best days, when I shake with fear.

Be content with that.

Over the tannoy, voices.

– A satirical and sceptical attitude to the conventional, an urge to turn it inside out, to distort it slightly in order to show the illogic of the usual.

– So Lenin, just like Tom, enjoyed the music hall?

– That's what Gorky says.

– I'm glad to hear it. What about Zurich Dada?

There's a knockling, scuffling noise as the microphone is handed on.

– Without organisation of the masses, the proletariat is nothing. Organised it is everything. Being organised means unity of action, unity of practical activity.

Thomas gets up to look at the grille in the carriage ceiling. Radio on the train? How is that possible? He staggers a little as the coach lurches into motion. His face swells and distorts under the CCTV lens, a study in incomprehension. A decorative border appears around his head. A male choir sings.

The workers said to Casey won't you help us win this strike?
But Casey said let me alone, you'd better take a hike.
Then someone put a bunch of railroad ties across the track.
And Casey hit the river with an awful crack.

Our hero's upturned features tilt and spin until they are displaced by a title card.

WHITSTABLE, A SMALL TOWN ON THE KENT COAST

– Go back to London? Preposterous idea.

– Porter. Porter! Here porter, dammit.

– I will remind you, sir, that we are first.

– Why weren't we warned about this?

– Here boy, over here.

– Bolsheviks. Agitators. Damnable rabble.

– Fat chance there'll be somewhere decent to stay.

– Can you pass a message to the Castle?

– Who's in charge? What is this place?

– Come back here at once I say.

As Tom and I step down on to the wind swept platform of a modern station, red brick dressed in blue, a cacophony of complaints breaks out around us.

The journey to Blackstable amused him, and, when they arrived, he was resigned and cheerful. Mrs Carey, knowing by what train they were coming, waited in the drawing room and listened for the click of the gate.

A salvo of yells erupts from the far platform.

– Stand with the miners!

– Not an hour on the day not a penny off the pay!

– Notter hour on the day notter penny off the pay!

– Notter hour!

– Yer not in London now yer bourgeois bigwigs!

Clustered at a gap between two carriages, angry passengers holler back at their hidden antagonists. Threats and retorts are lobbed between the brows of the wagons and the wooden teeth fringeing the canopy above their heads.

– We'll bring you Reds to your knees!

– Wanna try? Come over here Lord Pikey, let's 'ave yer.

– Shirkers! Resume your tasks or be replaced.

– Go back to Russia!

– Front me the fare I will.

– You don't scare us you corksackers!

– Impudence, the impudence. Barabbas! You are bandits!

– Ooooooh listen to Lady Five Fingers. Wankerrrrr!

From each side of the station, men with sticks are mounting the steps to a lattice footbridge which spans the line.

The station master, oil lamp in hand, locates us.

– This way sir sir, quickly now.

He takes us into his office.

– I'm sorry, gentlemen. The train will go no further tonight. There won't be another ahead of the morning. I have arranged accommodation for first class passengers in the town. Mr Luckhurst here will drive you.

– But I'm on my way to the Albemarle Hotel in Cliftonville. I need to get there.

– You will, sir, I'm sure of it. Though I do regret to say it won't be tonight. Threats have been made you see. The local garages are anxious for their vehicles. The drivers fear for their personal safety. We'll get you there tomorrow, there's no question about

From the summit of the station's coal heap, as powerful as fifty voices of other men, a stentor's battle cry cuts his promise short.

– Renationalise the railways!

Repeated and released from their moment, the words soar towards us over a freeze frame of carriages, disembarking passengers, and upended trunks. One, the director counts, and breathe. And two, and breathe, and three.

Cobbles of flung coal clatter on the canopy. Women shriek.

A huge hunk, primeval and perfectly pitched, shatters on the platform. Jags of black shrapnel burst like shot into the door of the office.

– Who larned yer to throw like that?

– Mills bombs mate. Life or death wern it.

– Cricket pitch on the Belmont more like.

– Bloody bulls eye!

– Time for the tub.

In the Labour Club I'm shown a photograph. It's tan brown, as if printed with tea. A shot of working men posing with a banner: Not a Penny Off the Pay. Their eyes are locked on the novelty of the camera, looking and learning. The director adds a voiceover, English with a Russian accent. He has the track ragged with static.

– Fog! Flow to the strikers as fresh milk. Turn into loaves of bread every cobble!

– Old Bill! Hop it lads!

Whistle blasts break out on all sides, in their wake the percussion of boots. The sepia figures drop their standard and scatter, exiting from the photograph frame right, frame left, frame front, holding on to their caps as they dash. When the police arrive all that remains is a pastoral scene, cottages and fields on Borstall Hill in the springtime. A cow grazes, ducklings and piglets wander freely, a young girl totters after geese. The constables remove their helmets. They load and light their pipes, taking their ease beneath the coppery trees.

– Eisenstein shot cattle in a slaughterhouse. Why don't we echo that?

– Because, my mad Leninista, England green and pleasant isn't Russia.

– Where do you think that menagerie came from?

– Ah. My bad.

– Dumbo.

Thomas paces up and down in the station master's office. He is exasperated. Blues and twos flash through the windows, swooping over the walls. The camera pans slowly to a tattered notice by the door. Tom's shadow beats upon the poster as he reads the words aloud.

– When he was come, as travellers are wont,

HE DID REPAIRE UNTO AN INNE

We are hurried through the hullabaloo and cackle of radios, the swift deployment of forces and the sparkling of lights.

Four of us board the taxi bound for town. Luckhurst is nervous and eager to leave. Our cases are roped swiftly to the rear. It's a flatulent ride, another horse scarer. I sit beside Thomas, facing forwards. He says nothing. One of his spats treads the other, both of his heels pedalling the air. His fingertips beat on a knee cap. He's jazz drumming in a chockfull dive on wheels, jittery and cornered.

The driver pipes up as we pass beneath the line.

– First railway bridge in the world, this one. For passenger trains.

I peer through the side window. Drab houses. A cricket pitch, a gasworks, the base of a stack, a small orchard. Terraces curtained with gloom shun the winking door of the Golden Lion.

Our companions for the ride are both in costume. Elaborate, but not incredible. One is dressed as a Chicago gangster. He has a plastic tommy gun and a facial scar made from gel. Tom thinks the other – in black jeans and a hooded top – is the more threatening of the two. He has a knife in his right hand. Is it real or plastic? His face is masked with a ghoulish scream.

– Are you on the way to a party?

– Nah mate, we always dress like this in Kent! You down from London?

– He kills me, your missus does. He's the one in fancy dress. Those shoes. That hat. Yer Fred the Shed ain't yer?

– Nyahahahahooh!

Capone levels the barrel of his weapon at Thomas. The scream raises his blade.

– We know what yer done. Empty aht yer pockets! Yer money or yer life.

– Our money or yer life!

– 'Undred per cent tax on the rich!

– Only jokin' Fred.

– Yeah, make it an 'undred and twenny!

– Nyahahahahoohooohooherahhahaha!

They are still laughing when they step out at the Railway Inn.

As the taxi pulls away, Thomas and I turn and look back.

Framed by the small rear window, enclosed within that by the frown of the bridge, the gangster bends and drops his pants, mooning a loon farewell. Above his bent form, backlit by the glow of the pub, a silhouette hand with a knife rises and plunges and rises and plunges.

Tom covers his face with his hands.

– It was an accident. She fell. Fanny fell.

Four words are chalked on the underside of the railway bridge. ESCAPE THERE IS NONE.

– You two all right back there? Hold on tight.

As we pass the junction with Cromwell Road the driver squeezes a large rubber bulb which is attached to a spiralling brass trumpet. The horn parps and parps, deafeningly. Purple erkle perple arkle. The taxi backfires like a shotgun, releasing a cloud of bubbles into the night. Much to Thomas's consternation, the doors begin to flap like wings. He leans out of the vehicle clutching at a leather straphandle, almost in then out of reach. For an instant I think he is trying to jump. I yank him back into his seat, saving him from a fall.

– That was close.

He doesn't respond.

– Could have killed yourself.

– I'm already dead. My heart is a handful of dust.

– Baloney. Let's see how things stand when we make the hotel.

– Believe me. I am already dead. It cannot be undone.

At that moment, caught by the wind, Tom's bowler frisbees back towards the junction. A boy in shorts catches the hat. He whistles and flicks it across to another brat on the opposite side of the street. Tom's door slams shut as the cab hits a bump in the road. The receiver skateboards past, slapping my door shut then handing off the hat to another scamp ahead of us. The third kid flags us down. The driver stops. Tom asks if I have any change. Instead of approaching the car the kid steps into the centre of the road a few feet ahead of us. He takes a claspknife from his pocket, opening it. He starts to sing at the top of his voice.

– Sheeeeeee stood there laughing. I felt the knife in my hand and she laughed no more. Forgive me Delilah I just couldn't take anymooooore.

He slashes the crown of Tom's hat into a toast rack.

– Did you see that? It's poetry, dramatic and epic. An emotion condensed.

– If you say so Tom. Who's Delilah?

– Have you understood nothing?

As we look on, the kid stamps on the slashed hat, swirls it in the dust with his foot, spits on it, picks it back up, and scarpers.

– OY!

The sketch ends with the yob running down a side street, bandy-legged and splayfooting, pursued by Tom waving his raised arms.

– Under the proper circumstances, murder can be comic.

Two minutes later Tom reappears with his hat intact. He is wearing the crooked tie and vagrant bags of the Tramp. The driver returns the cheery smile of the returning fare. As he starts to laugh, an intake of breath sucks the camera through a gap between two yellowing teeth. The lens pitches over a gum to reveal the smoky pit of his mouth, a pealing uvula swinging over the bloat of the throat below. Thomas clings to the fleshy clapper. His hat drops into the abyss, silk screaming silently as it plunges. Ding dong, toot toot, and off we go.

MISSING NAMES

As we pass Whitstable's largest cinema, the Oxford Picture Hall, the audience recognises the elaborate iron facade on the screen. There is loud cheering. Outside on the steps the uniformed commissioner salutes our cab as it goes by. The audience applauds his receding likeness.

– He's a nice fella Humphrey.

– Fanatical about the flickers.

– Three cheers for the hump!

Tom's face takes on a deathly hue – the green glow of an illuminated supermarket sign – as we approach the War memorial. Crosstipped and defended with iron rails, the monument gleams in light cast by our two weak headlamps. It throws an intense shadow, impossibly large and implausibly angled, on to the sheered building behind.

– Early Victorian those offices were. And soon to be demolished.

– Think Murnau, Wiene, Pabst. Think Lang.

– Looks like Batman to me.

At the meeting of the committee which was convened to decide what form the monument should take Mr F G Browning proposes a small latin crucifix atop a mercat cross of marble above an octagonal pillar of polished red granite from Aberdeen. He recommends that the pillar be mounted on a square gabled plinth on a grey granite base. Marble inventories of the Glorious Dead will be posted above three Yorkstone steps surrounding the base. The councillors agree.

In April 1921 Messrs Millen and Chrisfield of Faversham lay a granite base for a gabled plinth. They cage the stone with wooden scaffolds. Using three ropes, they raise a shaft of red marble. Between wagon and socket, the eight facets flash in the spring sun. The pillar is capped with a mercat cross then crowned with a latin roost. The scaffold is peeled away. Marble directories are attached. Yorkstone steps are placed around the base.

One hundred and seventy five names, and rising, are remembered with inscriptions. Controversy, corrections, and new bouts of slaughter drive up the total in the decades that follow Whitstable's erection of a ready reckoner for the dead.

– My nephew's name is missing. His pals are there, that fell with him in Flanders. People, by that I mean them that know, like the Federation of Demobilised Soldiers, they say there's a hundred more souls to go on the roll. A hundred. Council says they can't get every native on, but we must, it's only right. Cabbing brings me by ten times a day. You'll say I'm cracked, but I see him every pass, our Tommy. Saluting, standing on his hands, laughing with the lasses. Sometimes, at home, he cries at table. We love to hear him sing, me and the wife, when he's chopping us wood in yard. I get angry, oh I do, forgive me so. Held back from us in graves in Flanders where they're being forgot.

– I had a friend there too. I am sorry for your loss.

– One of too many, our one of many. An hundred and seventy five taken from this town alone, by rights maybe two hundred and seventy. I won't let it rest. He's a right to be on there. I'm hoping your friend made it back in one piece?

– He got through. I'm very fortunate that he did.

Dix from Dresden, Iron Cross second class, pauses halfway across a shadowy bridge in Camden. Reaching into his overcoat pocket, he unwraps a knife and tosses it into the Regent's Canal. Kerplupsh. As he walks on, he pitches again. A ripped page from the *Times Literary Supplement* – a crumpled assessment of the metaphysical poets – bobs like a marker buoy above the blade.

Coy Mistress felt by fits unbalanced struggle. Jonso. Dissociation, as is natural. The scrunched words sink beneath the scurf.

Streaming hair over stinging eyes, soggy shoulders over damp lapels. The orphans' necks are wet, the backs of their hands are wet, their shoes are sodden. Tears and drizzle douse the mourners at the first commemoration of the armistice. Within the rails, a drenched dress uniform, sopped robes of red. As they parade for Lord Harris GCSI GCIE CB – who exhibits no emotion – the fatherless children weep. Their backs are turned to the Coach and Horses, heads bent in rows, rain hosing their napes. I watch the first performance of the annual ritual from the pub's side window.

Six years before, Harris had harvested men at the Horsebridge, addressing crowds in the open air.

– The opinion of the civilised world is that we are at war for a just cause (Cheers). The German minister, when he protested against this country going to war, said 'surely you are not going to war for a scrap of paper', but it is something more than a scrap of paper because there is something on it and that is the name of England. It would be the same as a dishonoured cheque if we do not hold to our bond.

Roars of approval. Waves pause offshore. More roars. Cowed by the town, the evening tide stands down.

– England won't be bottom dog!

– We have an obligation!

– Let's go!

– Fight the just war!

– We'll bury the Hun!

A queue forms at the recruitment hall two hours before the door is due to open.

Four years later, the porch is draped with flags and bunting. Beery soldiers, drunken sailors spill from a honking coal truck that jaunts up and down the High Street. Depleted families wave from the roadside, smiling and mourning. Church bells ring Anglican gamelan without a pause. Bottles, barrels, pipe bowls are sucked till dry.

Lord Harris is attending a sitting of the East Kent Compensation Authority. Speaking for the Justices of the County, he refers to the joy they feel on the termination of the terrible incubus. He expresses their gratitude to the public.

– We have a grave sense of the loss which has been caused and a feeling of apprehension about the difficulties that lay before us.

At the second remembering by the ready reckoner, the leader of the council says:

– The bonds that bound us together are becoming ragged and frayed.

As I watch the decades timelapse, pride displaces grief. The mourners age and fall in number. Saplings rise and swell to trees, obstructing flags. They are lopped back. The great-great grandchildren of the dead and wounded prance to the whistles and drums of sea cadets. Preened and poppied mothers raise their phones. They snap and share proud parent moments. A newly chiselled corpse is a rare event.

For sixty years the taxi driver and his sister stand quietly to one side, their faces harrowed by their loss, wrinkled hands clasped, waning.

Tommy's name is still missing.

– Our God our help in ages past our hope for years to

The hymn is interrupted by a siren. A police van with a grille shielding its windscreen surges past the young standard bearers, engine gunning. The bonnet is dented. The sides are pocked black by thrown coal.

A war memorial is the still point around which a town turns, isn't it?

Tom is drumming again. A little further on the taxi passes between a church and a congregational hall. The two edifices stare each other down, theatrically, across the street. The church is retreating from the younger challenger. Shuttered shops alternate with public houses. We pass another picture palace. The driver points out a poster for tonight's programme – the actress Alice Brady gets HER GREAT CHANCE.

– It's a romance. A shop girl and a millionaire. My wife is all for going. Have either of you seed it? Myself, I'd rather go to Famine, about Red Russia, poor starving souls. Not mother's cup of tea at all. So Her Great Chance it is.

Strollers, tarts and drunks, so many. A mud pusher. Former soldiers, some missing limbs. A legless torso on a tray hauls himself forward with ragbound hands. Shadowy prefigurings. Then, where the road forks, a gaslamp, a garage called Wood's, and two hotels.

– Whitstable is the harbour of Canterbury. It is celebrated for its oyster fishery, the produce of which, under the name of natives, is highly esteemed in London and other markets. The town, though rather mean in appearance, and irregularly built, has a bustling and thriving appearance, from its fishing and coal trade.

That's how Bradshaw set the scene. It will do.

The driver pulls up a few yards short of the Duke of Cumberland. Lemon brick dressed cherry, the hotel is like a giant gift box fastened with red ribbon, a gaudy three storey birthday present delivered to a grey address in error.

– The Duke's the superior of the two sir. Plush and pleasing they say. I wouldn't know. Many calls it the Butcher.

– The Butcher? Why's that?

– Culloden sir.

Thomas strides towards the brightly lit building without a word, leaving me to settle the fare and to lug his baggage across the dung-spudded intersection. We're going to have words, Tom and I.

I watch Luckhurst unrope the suitcase. I hand over two bob and wait as he searches, unwillingly, for change. As my back was turned I'm not sure which door Tom used to enter the hotel.

Following him in today I scan the ceiling for clues to the old configuration of rooms and entrances. The interior walls which divided the ground floor were torn out long ago. The public areas have changed beyond recognition. Thomas probably came in directly from the high street, centre front, and up the low rise steps. If he fancied a stiff drink – given the events of the last few hours who could blame him – he may have taken the corner door and made his way to the saloon. Then again, he may have looked the place over, walking into Harbour Street before entering under the gas lamp that still curlicues over the ceramic porch. The truth is Thomas could have entered from any direction. It's a pub. It wasn't designed to keep people out.

The manager steps forward to greet him.

– Good evening sir. Ah yes indeed, the station master spoke to us by telephone. I'm extremely sorry that your journey has been interrupted. These strikes discredit the town. He was very fortunate to secure a room. An electrical engineer for a company contriving pictures decamped at short notice, summoned back to London by a telegram. Their shoots, as they call them, are a source of great excitement here. Mr Roscuro was the lighting skip but his deputy is competent and the dawn sortie – so to speak – is en plain d'air so Mr Hayes, the director, agreed to release him. Though he was not entirely happy to do so, as one might expect. It's a well-appointed room, nine shillings for the night, sixteen full board.

– I'm very fortunate. And very grateful. I wonder, could I ask you to contact the manager at the Albemarle? I was due there tonight. Trade winds have stalled my progress. Je m'en fus alors a Whitstable. Could you explain?

– At once sir.

He signs the register, a huge tome. February 18th 1922. Thomas Stern.

That guest book is now missing. Long lost. A vital piece of evidence, it was never secured by Sergeant Winchell, an oversight he would greatly regret.

I have searched for it in the files of barristers, in the attics of retired publicans, and in brewery basements. I have visited municipal archives, and clicked through online databases. The register has vanished without trace.

It's as if Thomas Stern was never here.

The ledger must have disappeared before midnight, certainly by lunchtime the next day, or the police would surely have seized it. Tom seems to have had an accomplice, hastily recruited, here in Whitstable too.

I have three suspects. A police officer, Bill Janes, who was deployed on the case but later employed by Stern in a private capacity. Conan, the assistant manager, an oddball with airs, who was responsible for the guest book and accounts. And one Joan Cade, an obliging maid, who we will meet shortly.

By disposing of the only record of the stopover, Tom's local aide, whoever it was, dealt a severe blow to the town's economy.

Whitstable's enterprise network recently calculated that documentary evidence of Stern's visit would have benefited local traders by at least £250,000 annually – that's twelve and a half million in total – in the five decades since his death.

The scale of those lost revenues persuaded the local business community to meet the costs of my reopening the case. They calculated the proceeds from a marketing drive, events, merchandise, possibly an annual festival marking Stern's visit to the town, would rapidly dwarf my fee. There was one condition. I must carry out my research discreetly and do nothing to damage the reputation of Whitstable.

I wonder. When, exactly, did Tom book the Albemarle?

I sit in the Duke's foyer with my notebook, watching, straining to hear the voices, recording every scrap of conversation I can catch. I see them and they see me.

The proprietor's voice is oily and eager to please.

– You're from America, sir? I did think so. I believe you call this 'checking in' at home. Which is, if I may ask? Ah, St Louis. Marvellous.

A business card glides across the mahogany.

– I say. Lloyds, Colonial and Foreign, in Lombard Street. A City man. We've a new branch here ourselves sir, only a few steps away. Stearling, the manager, will be in later. He opened a year ago. The bank is certainly a force in the land. Down from London for the air? For our oysters perhaps? They are a draw. Well, not ours, not this year sadly. We have supplies from Maldon. From the other side. Of course sir, at what time? This young man will show you to your room. A maid will be along shortly.

Here and for now, it seems, they don't know who Thomas really is. He appears to be safe for tonight . If he is discovered I expect he will outrun his pursuers, pull a Charlie and sham a lampstand. I cross the road to the cheaper hotel.

– He was a pretty one, wasn't he, the porter? And she was no slouch either.

– I'll take your word for it. I didn't get much of a look.

– You expect me to believe that?

– I didn't take much notice.

– Really? You'll never make a detective.

I climb the stairs to the second-floor room, front, that I had booked online. I drop my bag on the bed and move the only chair to the window.

Figures drift through the Cross below me, shadowed by my questions. What is Tom's plan? And state of mind? Why does he say he is dead? What does he think will happen next? He cannot believe his actions will have no consequence. And where does that confidence in Otto come from?

Four roads and an alley converge here. The main drag arrives from the left, forking at the Duke into Sea Street and Harbour Street. Kick a ball in Terry's Lane, opposite my window, and you might score in the passage to my left, Knots Yard. The Cross is like a dried starfish trodden into the dust of the town.

Solitary figures, with time on their hands, air their heels below my window. Others, with money in their pockets, hurry towards the lights. Now and then a couple step out with purpose. Gaggles stream to guzzle at rendezbooze.

I can see into the bar of the Duke. A murmur rises like a beehive's hum. I use my binoculars to read the lips of the nearest customers. They are discussing dragons in a den, daughters and weddings, the moolah to be had from architectural salvage, last week's footie scores. Bets have been placed, bets have been lost, the caravan is leaking, there's a queue at the crossing and a tailback that is longer at junction two. They're having a good one.

– See the rack on that? That's my supper.

– That that is a person, mate.

– Piss off you peecey pussy.

– World class band this Thursday but the bass player's crap.

– Beer me, I'll pay yer back then.

As the night goes on I've got that, I liked that and I want one too. Love that album adore that pink top. I need chips now. Eleven hundred cc between my knees fifteen per cent discount and a week off what's not to like. Abba tribute tickets going for a song, ready for another holiday, been there, no not me, flagging and surging, postponing the end.

Local colour. Work in all you know. Make them accomplices.

Leakage from the word hoard being carried up the stairs.

Lines soon to be banned, with arrest a certainty for anyone flogging greek blue. Sergeant Winchell will whoop for joy tomorrow when he discovers that all 732 pages of Joyce's delinquency are in his captive's bag.

– My enquiries, sir, reveal that Thomas Stern, detained for the murder of his wife Frances, is a leading member of an international publishing conspiracy which promotes and distributes licentious and prohibited literature. The moral, aesthetic and indeed the spiritual disturbance of the realm is the explicit purpose of their shared undertaking. Educated pornographers, sir, that's what they are. Decadent despite appearances, highbrow and mostly atheistical. I believe Stern's wife stumbled on the truth and paid the ultimate price.

– You're going to base your case on that baloney?

– On reflection, sir, probably not. I have been through Stern's papers. Poetry is Stern's priority, the only thing that matters to him. He believes, fervently, that personal feeling and emotion have to be sacrificed for free verse to succeed. I think that's why he killed her.

– So you're saying composition was his motive?

– In a manner of speaking, sir. In order to escape from his personality.

– Are you out of your mind Winchell?

– There is another possibility. We found medical bills in the apartment.

– Your point, sergeant?

– A number of the invoices are outstanding. I believe he murdered his wife to save thousands of pounds in doctor's fees.

– It's a pleasure, Winchell, to follow the working of a keen mind. You may proceed.

Thomas follows the concealed crime up to the first landing. Eye level, it slaps cheek on cheek above the porter's thigh. Heads turn as the figure sitting in the row behind me speaks.

– How hard it is to climb another man's staircase.

– SSShhhhhhhhhssssh!

– Take your step and find your foothold.

At the second turning of the stair Thomas spies a maid following below. A cap, a frill, a sweep of blue. He won't be alone with the porter after all.

He has always felt pursued. It's a conviction that will never lapse.

Most of the natives I interview about the stopover and capture of Thomas will confuse today's events with another killing, one committed seven miles away in Canterbury on land laid waste by war and teeming with cats. Few recall anything that happens tonight. Some will insist, against all the evidence and disregarding his confession, that Stern committed no crime at all.

– You see, it is only suspicion so far. We have nothing to go upon.

– It was an accident. She fell.

– On a knife?

– Facts are stubborn things, Mr Stern. Whatever may be our wishes, our inclinations, or the dictates of our passion, they cannot alter the state of facts and evidence.

– But it was an accident.

Boy, bag, Thomas, maid, ascending. Residents and waiters congest the first-floor corridor, a squeeze gut alley twenty feet above the bar. Discreet knocks announce room service at the doors of couples never seen in public.

– A cauldron of unholy loves.

– Beg pardon sir? Here we are.

The porter unlocks the door.

Tom's words about the cauldron, I think I invented those. Either that or the maid, who was close behind, told me about them later. Much later, even decades later. My notes are unclear and my version control was poor. My memory is beginning to let me down.

But he said it, of that I am fairly certain.

The sound of a page being turned.

FUGITIVE AT THE CROSS

Thomas tells the maid to come back later. He follows the young man into the bedroom. It has two sets of arched windows, one pair to the right, overlooking the garage, and another to the front, giving a view up the main street. A taxi is approaching with more passengers rescued from the station.

– They crease me up, those two. My nephew's one of the fallen.

A street lamp stands at the centre of the junction. Beside it there is a box truck draped with posters lettered in red: FAIR RATE FOR LOCAL HEROES. The wooden arms of the cart are propped on a carpenter's trestle.

– There may be some disturbance from the Cross tonight sir.

The porter stands, hands clasped behind his back, in the middle of the room.

– Why's that, my boy?

– The Labour Party has called a public meeting. Their numbers grow by the week.

– What do they want?

– Work. With reward sufficient to support their families.

Tom steps towards the boy and places a hand on his shoulder.

– Don't hold back.

– The council has provided employment on the sea wall for some of the two hundred men registered at the Labour Exchange. At first the government agreed to provide funds but the minister has withdrawn from any commitment. Unless a loan can be raised, the town's ratepayers will have to stump up. It's either that or see the scheme shut down. The men are on strike anyway, for tenpence an hour, which they say is the proper rate. The poster speaks to both meanings of the dispute. A fair rate. I think it's clever.

– You are sympathetic to the cause?

– They are entitled to a hearing. Most of the councillors are downstairs now, in the saloon. The town is very divided on the issue.

He hands the room key to Thomas.

– They used to meet in the old hotel that stood here. Organised labour,

I mean. Before the rebuilding. No longer, of course. Mr Slawson, our governor, would never allow it. He refuses to allow the socialist candidate, Lieutenant Colonel Sims, on the premises.

– I'm not surprised. Now tell me. What must one see when in Whitstable?

The boy points to a dredgerman's hall through a side window. He describes the eighteenth-century assembly room that faces it, an oriel window nearby, and the figurehead from a ship, overlooking the estuary.

– The Painted Lady. From the Chance. She went down in fifty-seven.

– Very informative. Got a name have you?

– Mathias.

– You seem to know this place from top to bottom, Matt.

Thomas taps the young man on the tip of his nose.

– From your cute little top. To your bellboy butt.

He strokes the boy's rump.

Mathias doesn't respond. He waits for a coin.

– Are we going to release deleted scenes? I nominate this one.

– Gay Tom's just speculation, isn't it?

– No idea. I'm not a NEP man and I don't like girls.

– Come again?

– Only the comic cuts.

– Which are?

First up, the set for the apartment in Crippens Court Gardens. Fanny stands over Tom who is seated, cutting open the pages of a new book. Action. She palms his forehead. A close up of Tom's face, surprised. He retorts, silently. Fanny walks away. She trips on the rug. Staggering, she spills her drink down her dress. She bursts out laughing. Tom stands up, honking too. A blooper. Fanny, shaking her head, leaves the shot, an assistant dabbing at her with a towel. A set carpenter smoothes the rug and nails its edge down. Tom approaches the camera and gurns into the lens.

He sits down on the bed.

– You're such a bluenose Matt. I expect you've been told that before.

– I were thinking if he touches me again, I'll put his fucking lights out.

– It comes with the job son. Stand your ground they'll leave you alone.

I snoop from across the street. Tom holds out a coin – how much? – a tanner probably. Or a piqued thruppence. The door closes. He locks it immediately.

A quick inventory. Armchair, wardrobe, chest, bed. On the first night of their honeymoon Fanny trashed their room. Tom kipped in a deckchair on the beach. There's dust here too, of course. A veil of dust and a bowl of rose leaves.

Eregeek. Greebeek.

Across the road to his left a hanging sign rasps in gusts from Harbour Street. A brown bear shouldering a key, creaking dismally as it paddles through the squall.

Erbscgreek, sgreek. A horse opera, the opening shot. A killer's lidless eyes, shaded by the brim of his stetson. Two outlaws in the Spanish west, shooters holstered, rifles cradled, wait for a train to arrive. It won't be long. We hear the locomotive's whistle in the distance. A windpump wheel scrapes and squeaks in the breeze. The London train whistles as it pierces the town. The banditti check their revolvers. The film has been unspooling for four minutes. Hardly a word has been spoken but the audience in the Coliseum is on the edge of its seat. Ereek. Eregreek. The *musique concrète* which opens *Once Upon A Time in the West* plays here, after sundown, at the Cross. Keep your heads down y'all.

Above the groaning sign, from a first floor window in the facing hotel, a woman looks across at Thomas. She dances, unaccompanied, in the room below mine. I'm told she unbuttoned her blouse.

Thomas sees her through his own reflection in the window. The dancer has Fanny's shoulders. Her hips too. At this distance he can hold her whole in the palm of his hand. Or seat her in the crook of his arm. It was just a push.

The woman points down, towards the entrance to her hotel. She beckons Tom across with a finger. She tugs the curtains shut.

– All around me a cauldron.

Does he stay or does he go? He stays.

He stands by the foot of the bed. Once he had walked in on Bertie, arched over Fanny on the bolster. Her startled stare beneath a nod of greeting. Bertie's closing drumroll. I am vitally needed there, he would write.

– He was fucking my wife.

– What did you do? What did you say?

– We never spoke about it afterwards, not ever. I got my letter in first. As to your coming to stay the night at the flat when I am not there, such a concession to conventions never entered my head. My very words. I rolled over. Pure and simple. I didn't have much choice.

– How did it end?

– He dumped her of course. After three years. Left her suicidal. There were smudges of blood on one of Bertie's forearms. A surprise visit from granny. Fanny's intimates always risked a splatter. She flipped one night in Eastbourne. She insisted we had to take the soiled bedding home with us. I smuggled the sheets on to the train and sent them back in a parcel.

The grisly linen was crammed into the case now yawning on the hotel bed.

Sergeant Winchell will find incriminating stains on the lining tomorrow.

After an hour skirting around the question, Thomas will concede that the smears on the underside of the lid are blood and the blood is that of his wife.

– All right, yes, yes, it's hers. Fanny's.

– You admit that the stains on the valise are blood? The blood of the victim? At last. Now we are getting somewhere. Evidence, Mr Stern, stubborn facts. So may I draw your attention to the cover of the book? What blots are these?

Winchell will pile the evidence high, raising a Calvary for our terrified bankbard.

But not tonight.

– I was alone in my room and undetected. That was something to be grateful for. But for how long? To be thus is nothing, but to be safely thus. I had no idea what was going on in London. Or what might happen next. Was Otto acting on my note?

Dix disguised Fanny's corpse with tattoos. The tramp stamps are clearly legible in the painting. Knives and keys bearing names. A lion grappling with a bear. The insignia of a regimental whore. The redbrick buildings beyond the window look to me like Dresden, where Dix roomed as a student before the war. The scheming staff sergeant was smart. He concealed Tom's crime in an upmarket brothel in Saxony.

Winchell will know nothing of the painter and his drawings, of the canvas and the diary, until I disclose them.

– My questions all boil down to one Mr Stern.

– I know. You're asking did I kill my wife.

– Did you?

– I'm not the type.

As I carry the lustmord to my home in Sea Street, I pass between the site of the bankrupt garage and the Duke of Cumberland, directly beneath the windows of Thomas's room. Looking up at the blank face of the hotel I wave a fist and shout.

– Here, at last, is the evidence which will convict you.

Heads turn. A Japanese tourist snapping the gaudy facade of Wheeler's, a heritage seafood joint, turns her camera on me instead. A greasemonkey looks up from a winged bonnet. I shout again. I cannot make myself heard.

Thomas is unpacking, transferring books from his bag to the bedside table. Middleton. The copy of *The Mysterious Affair* which I lent him. Cut and uncut pages newly arrived, bluebound, from Paris. He sits by a window and slits more of the page blocks open.

As he rips through the doubled sheets with a knife, the hotel room grows darker. Three rows of cornered words resist the fade, enlarging to fill the screen.

MOURNING MASTERS
MEET SERGEANT GOB

Winchell turns on the tape recorder. Crossing his legs he leans back in his seat.

– Would you please tell us your name and occupation sir, and how you know Mr Stern?

– My name is Hephaistos. I live and work in Sheffield. I'm the master at the Avalon Forge. Amongst other things, I craft knives for heroes.

– Other things, sir?

– Wings for helmets, armour for the Gods, thrones.

– What is your relationship to Thomas Stern?

– Thomas is a regular customer. He knows his cuttle. He's a discriminating buyer with an eye for good pieces, not somebody who will be satisfied with a cheap pigsticker. Cold-rolled stainless steel with a machine finish, that's for the plebs, Thomas won't touch it. The small one, the chiv you say you took from his pocket, that's a twca. If you walk around a church seven times with one of those, your partner for life will appear, bearing a sheath for the blade. That's how he met his wife. A lark during a party. The knife in the plastic pouch, which appears to have blood on it, is an adamantine. Perseus used the prototype to behead Medusa. Remember that case? It's worth a look. Now let's see. Thomas is, at this very moment, using a Carnwennan to fillet Ulysses. That's a dagger I forged for King Arthur. It's the smart device of custom knifemaking. A Carnwennan shrouds its handler in shadows. It's one of Tom's favourites. They sell well online. This one, the Morgul-blade hidden in the suitcase lid, is a very special piece. Did you know it was there? It's poisonous. It's never been used. Stab someone with one of these and the weapon turns to dust. Except for the tip. That little bugger detaches the instant it touches flesh. Then it tunnels straight for the heart. It's a real labour-saver, that widget. It won me a bundle of awards, attracted venture capital. Gave me a pension too. Last but not least, the blade with the black handle. That's as blunt as a lead pipe. If you put it under your pillow it will keep nightmares away. I imagine Tom could use one tonight.

– Are you a registered cutler, sir?

Yesterday I found a rubber knife on the floor of a taxi in Shoreditch. The driver laughed.

– Chuck it here, mate. I know where that comes from. Costume hire on

Tabernacle Street. I'll drop it back. I remember the pair what had it, Capone and the Scream, a double act, they creased me up they did.

Thomas stops slicing. I step back from my window. He surveys the darkening high street from his roost. We both look down the corridor of moving shadows, a furrow puddled with lamplight, spangled here and there with uncurtained panes.

– It may not be Cliftonville, but tonight it will have to do.

– Their loss our gain dearie. Without the bleedin' strike we wouldn't have met would we?

– I suppose not.

– Coming back for puddin'? Or you gonna read me another poem?

Looking down into the Cross, Tom recognises a figure carrying a large, flat package wrapped in brown paper and tied with string. The man had lent him a book on the train and later shared a taxi with him. The pedestrian looks up. He also recognises Thomas. He shouts excitedly, pointing at the package with his free hand, stabbing at the wrapping with a finger.

– There's no hiding from this! I've got you now.

When I realise Thomas can't hear me, I continue towards the warehouse.

He resumes the sliding and the slicing, the regular rip of the paper the only sound and the sole movement in the unshared room.

/

A fairy boy of eleven, a changeling, kidnapped…

/

/

He sets the book aside and takes out a typed report on the liquidity of French banks. Beside that he places a clutch of newspaper cuttings on the syndicalist movement in Paris, in Lyons and other major cities. Bankslog. The usual homework. Tom is behaving as if nothing remotely lifechanging took place in north London only three hours ago. The work routines of the City have an amnesiac side effect.

For six days each week, in a boxroom off a back corridor, in a chamber with a view of the Mansion House, facing the clock of St Mary Woolnoth, in a burrow beneath the footslabs of the City – wherever he happens to be deployed – Thomas updates the balance sheet of war. He monitors financial transfers, the streams of francs and marks that transmute into Sterling, reparations imposed at Versailles, paybacks from Paris, banque disbursements, tresorraum transfers, compensation from the Finanzministerium, carefully logging them all into ledgers at Lloyds.

A conscientious tallyman, he has a quick eye for anything that might delay remittances, trigger defaults, or stem flows. Soles pad across the ceiling, past the door, beneath the window, the six day long. Pad, pad, strikes in the ports, pad pad, the tack of brolly tips, pad pad, spikes in cash withdrawals, pad pad, the rising crack of hobnails. Red-eyed scavengers step out with boorish creepers. A conger eel of clerks arches like a bridge. The imbecility of the Britisher. The putresecent literature and journalism of their capital city.

– Theirs, not mine.

– You're sure?

– That's what he wrote. I've checked.

– Stern is an alien. He is widely travelled. For what purpose, we must ask ourselves? A bank position offers good cover to espionage. What are this man's real loyalties, with whom do they lay?

Sergeant Winchell is meticulous. The investigation will be thorough. A crime has been committed. Every page must be used for the collection, selection and combination of evidence. On the authority of the perpetrator.

– What was behind it all? There was something, I now felt sure. He had a secret which he was cunningly trying to hide. There would be no rest for me until I had found out.

Can we put a finger on anything, the smallest thing, and say this we know?

The elegant prostitute that night on the Rue Sebastopol, what had she said?

– Monsieur, madame, nothing matters here except the franc. Toute le reste est de la fumée.

Everything else is smoke, like the trail she leaves, sashaying through the jazz-cooled night from Avenue Laforgue on to Rue Djuna. The following week, over tea and scones, Thomas repeats her words to senior colleagues at the bank. He implies that his source is highly placed, very well connected in the second arrondissement. He adds a punchline of his own.

– Nothing matters in Paris except the franc, that is their fundamental position. Toute le reste est de la fumée. A bitter smoke, no doubt, but smoke.

He has a bilingual slice of The Divine Comedy in his coat pocket, now as then as always. He snacks on the compact pages daily, feeding his fear of life after death.

– I'm a week away from the deathless summit.

– You're a walking bloody library Tom.

Fanny leaps to her feet.

– Without your books you're bloody spineless.

A bang on the wall. Two bangs on the wall, two that became one.

– I pushed her.

They will surely know by now. They must be on to me by now. Surely.

Tom moves his chair to a window above the Cross. A small crowd is forming by the box cart, obscuring the poster. He opens a notebook and writes:

> *Middleton understood women better than any of the Elizabethans. The changeling. Horror and comedy with no sentiment. There is no message.*

There is a hair on the page, a brown hair, inkdragging, caught in the nib of the pen.

Whose? And what does he mean, no message?

Tom will write at a later date:

> *I had always supposed, wherever I went, that she would be with me. Whatever I did, that she was unkillable.*

He looks down on the muster again. It is growing. Above the swarm the bear is restless, its key glinting in the windowlight. Tom frowns as the puzzle flaps in the breeze.

– How will I sleep through that?

The image perplexes him. No one, he thinks, has argued that a bear holds the key to knowledge or to salvation. No bear ever got its paws on the key to the abyss. Not even that grizzler in Daniel, the one with three ribs in its mouth. Something to do with the stars perhaps? The Great Bear. Or Russia, maybe Russia and the future of Europe?

That's stretching it. This is a coastal town. Think local.

– A gay thing?

– No. The Bubble's a port.

– It has a harbour?

– Cargo coming in and out.

– It's a corruption. A bear on the quay. Of course! A dancing bear to draw salts and clods to the alepump.

A curtain immediately above the sign, the curtain of the window below mine, is pulled to one side. Thomas steps back.

– It was my next door neighbour from Paddington. I'm sure of it. The painter. Sheila something.

The director calls for a pause.

– We're taking this out. Delete it.

But as the sergeant will say tomorrow

– In cases like this, there's no such thing as coincidence.

Is that my wife's laughter I hear beneath my feet?

Down in the Cross something has changed. The crane unit shows the crowd taking a new shape. The man who passed through earlier with a package has returned. A ragged crescent forms around him. The zoom reveals he's chanting. There are too many people in the way. I can't make out his words. He thrusts a placard up towards Tom's window. It has four words on it.

BUM ON THE PLUSH

Tom yanks his curtains shut. That's not a welcome development. I cross over to the Duke of Cumberland and sit alone in the bar, reading and hoping that he will come back down. I am worried the trail may go cold. But Tom will want to eat, I'm fairly sure of that.

Musicians are setting up on a stage at the back of the hotel. Behind them bulbs embedded in black chipboard spell out THE DUKE. A pensioner in aged denim sings a soundcheck.

– Last night I got loaded. On a bottle of whiskey, on a bottle of bearkeyshhhwhmph...

Overloaded circuits burr and buzz. Unplugged he's a frail peep.

– I feel all...

– Hold it, hold it Jim. Wait up. Ok. Again.

– Bottle a whiskey. An I feel all right. And I feel all rye, eye, ite.

Sergeant Winchell would like this song. It would have been a good number for Marie Lloyd too, flirting on the stage at the Victoria Palace, parasol swirling, bottle swinging, swaggering and swigging and nodding the wink.

– That collaboration of the audience with the artist which is necessary in all art.

– And I feel all rye, eye, ite.

Gerruzzzzzghgrrrrrmmmmbawk.

The sound check is riven by a shriek of feedback. The musicians look at each other in mock alarm. They did it to get attention, for a laugh, for no reason at all.

Moving to the next mike, the singer begins to ramble about a millenarian figure on a white horse and a loaf of bread hoisted on a pitchfork

– So Courtenay addressed the oystermen on the beach. He told them about hunger in the villages. He denounced the landowners of the county. Rise up, get off your knees with me, he said, for we are invicta. Behold the white horse. There on the hill, in Bossenden Wood, the murderer Knatchbull rode them down. Our men were shot like game. Our Glorious Dead. It is right to rebel¸ as the helmsman said. Smash the four olds. Bombard HQ. Don't forget what the dormouse said. Feed your head. One two, one two.

The gossip market is a noisy place. Nobody listens to his gibberish except me.

Thomas is greeted by the waiter. He selects a table to the left of space taken by the band. Cacti, each pot labelled by genus – discocactus, isolatocereus, mamillaria, parodia, stetsonia – line a shelf beneath a window that overlooks the yard.

The denim prophet lifts a speaker on to the stage so Tom can be seated.

– Fight the good fight!

– mm mm mm mm

Tom hums to the chorus coming from the front of the hotel. The waiter returns.

– It's the public meeting, sir. To make the men's views better known to the councillors. It's much quieter back here.

– A remarkable collection.

– The cacti? They are an enthusiasm of the owner, sir. He's a prickly fellah, Mr Slawson. Ha! The Duke of Cactusland we sometimes call him. A sharp tongue he has. Duck of Cucumberland too, when he's in his cups. Not to his face of course, oh no, we're nay daft, oh no. What would sir like to order?

Framed by the window a horse, warblind and blinkered, clopsparks over the cobbles. A stable lad steers the beast's flared bulk around a delivery van from which a large flat screen television is being unloaded. A double decker hurtles past the open gate, its lights silhouetting a figure pushing a wooden handcart that is piled high with dung. His legs and spine are braced at nine twenty. Today's street harvest – on its way to a market garden on Borstall Hill – has been crowned with a saucepan. A troubadour tunes his lute in the gloom.

The man behind me in the cinema leans forward and whispers

– It is quite obvious that we do not all of us inhabit the same time.

– It is quite obvious to me that we do.

– We don't.

– We do.

– This is going nowhere.

– Can we agree on a point of intersection?

– Shshshhhhhhh!

In the dining room, in the yard, in the auditorium, here on the page, wherever and whenever we read, we experience the simultaneity of the non-simultaneous.

Tenses are mythologies, futile attempts to fix time and sequence, faked coordinates for points that do not exist. Tense past and tense future present as imperfect.

– What's your source? Do the dates tally?

– It's pastiche. Don't underrate it.

The two musicians walk over for a closer look at Tom. One of them fingers a sleeve. He's intrigued by the chained cuff links, the tie pin. The other waddles like a penguin, arms tight to his sides, chuckling. He blubbers and holds out his wrists to be cuffed. Shaking their heads and laughing they both return to the stage. Thomas ignores them. He opens a book.

Did he know that we suspected him, I wondered. Surely he could not be unaware of the fact, conceal it as we would. Did he feel some secret stirring of fear, or was he confident that his crime would go unpunished? Surely the suspicion in the atmosphere must warn him that he was already a marked man.

I leave the set briefly to buy a drink. A motionless couple are startled by my shadow as it dapples their table. The barman hands me a folded note with my change. It has six words on it. I can feel dimples with my fingertips, nooks beneath my thumb. The message has been typed. The pensioner coughs and taps a mike, preparing to sing the content. The phrase appears on screen like a karaoke prompt. Each word heads the ball to a teammate standing in front of it.

LAST NIGHT I GOT LOW DEAD

– Onabot love whiskey. Onabot love whiskey. Anna feel all right. Nafeel all right. Rye eye ight.

The waiter delivers a dozen bivalve molluscs to Tom at his table. Oysters on exoskeletons over crushed ice on chrome are plunked on a composite mat sealed with a fading publicity shot of Tankerton Slopes. The cloth has a nautical theme – ship's wheels, gurning sharks and seashells. It shrouds a ring-stained table made from offcuts of Burma teak. Each of the four legs is balanced on a single copper toe. On the top tier of this motley scaffold the oyster meat glisters, slowbroiling in the onstage lighting.

– From the other side sir, I'm sorry to say. We do concede their quality.

In Paddington the neighbour is on edge, his ear to the wall. For more than two hours there have been no slams, no raised voices, no judders or hissing of pipes, no creaks no thuds no brash invasive gramophone to indicate that anyone is in the apartment next door.

– Something's wrong. Listen.

– I can't hear anything.

– That's what I mean.

A constable explains how the body was discovered.

– Billeted beside the Sterns, a bad-tempered brace who peck at each other constantly, even when they're kipping, he could never be certain that quiet periods would last. The evening was unnaturally silent. The calm is worse than the storm, he says, when you're expecting the rhythmic grumbles. It sounded as if nobody was in, but he knew Mrs Stern hadn't left the building. Could she be sleeping, he asked his wife. It was possible. They had both, on more than one occasion, smelt morphine syrup on her breath.

– The stillness, that's why I knocked on the door. The apartment was far too quiet, unnaturally quiet. We were concerned for Fanny.

– I went to the flat because I'd received a telegram from Mrs Stern. I only went there because of the bloody telegram. How many times do I have to tell you?

– Course I let myself in. I do for them. I've got my own key.

Thomas answers my tap at the door.

– I'm sorry to intrude. Tom. Can I remind you the walls are rather thin? Sometimes we hear every word. We try not to, of course, but short of sitting with our fingers in our ears, like Quakers in a church, we can't avoid it. You do know that, don't you?

– Please accept my apologies. Fanny isn't well.

– I'm sorry to hear that.

– We had a tiff, a contretemps. She is very upset. I'm sorry we've spoiled your evening.

The disturbed tenant returns to his apartment. Tom closes the door. Husband and wife embrace before addressing the camera.

– I loved him in a way that destroyed us both.

– I loved her the more because I had mangled her.

– I was unwell much of the time.

– The marriage gave no happiness to her.

– I was a drag on him.

– Poetry was an escape from emotion.

I am Arnaut, who weeps and goes singing; grieving I see my past folly, and I see rejoicing the joy I hope for before me.

In the stable beside the hotel, the horseboy spits on strips of jingling leather tackle. He waxes, he wipes, he shines. When the straps are riding nails in the wall, the yard intendent will release him to walk the three miles home.

The waiter places a water jug, glazed carrot, on the table.

– They are from Maldon, on the other side of the estuary. The oysters. Forriners not natives, sad to say. The competition is temporarily in the ascendant. We have no supply of our own this year.

– They do look appetising.

– Down from London sir? I imagined so. We always get a few heralding the season, flits from the timekept city, bolting the old brown fog. Now and again one fails to get the last train back. A young lady walked into the sea at the West Beach only last week. Londrowners, we call them. Drown from Cockneyshire for the day. Why do they come to Whitstable to croak? Does our coroner place advertisements in the *Evening News*? Inquest and chips. A banquet on the beach is the best bequest. A little bit of humour helps, I find, don't you? Humankind cannot bear very much reality.

Tom doesn't answer. He has stopped eating and is scribbling in his notebook.

In Paddington the officers are leaving the apartment. As they descend the stairs their capes slap against the balustrade. The dining chair is no longer on its back. The floating witnesses have gone. Ambulance porters are lifting Fanny's body on to a stretcher. The landlord is standing by the door. The neighbour cannot get to sleep. All of the men wear one grim face.

In the back rows of the Oxford Street Picture House deceptively motionless couples are caressing discreetly. Hands check hands, hands free hands, hands steer hands in a dralon furrow of silent negotiations. Cautious loosenings get underway. The first unlacing is complete. The eyes of the paramours are fixed upon the screen. As the wounds of the murdered woman flash by, as knives rip, as orphans mourn, as sod slaps on to a coffin and the landlord bows his head, young pulses are galloping, doubts have deliquesced. Questing palms surf in sweat.

In Hammersmith the Palais is perkling. In Victoria the throats of the Palace Theatre are raw with song. In Whitstable the dining area in the Duke fills as rock buffs and dancefloor dames move in from the bar to take their seats. They line the walls in tribal pecking order, him, her, that, her mate, that lot, them, whatsisname. DFLs, down from London. They thread their way through the tables, forming a semicircle around Thomas and the stage as they wait for the band to start.

– Is there anything else I can get you sir?

Thomas shakes his head and raises an oyster, solitary in the deserted dining room. Grudge not the oyster. Smooth creatures, expiring, with the strong salt taste of living things under the sea. Ostreidae dressed in stiff saliva. Stab the shuck deep into the hinge. Twist. Force the blade up it. Slash through the living muscle. Swallow.

Here, again, I bring death.

Surrounded by crowd, I watch Tom mollusc by the window.

The neighbour will still be listening. The neighbour is always listening. He hears the officers examine each of the rooms in the neighbouring apartment. One calls down to another stationed on the doorstep.

– No one to enter, nobody to leave.

Muffled voices seep through the wall.

– We'll track him down. Don't you worry sir. We'll catch up with him.

– We caught Crippen dinnent we. We'll catch this Yank too.

– He'll swing. You'll see.

– Yessir, he will. He'll dance the Paddington frisk for sure.

Six empty, one raised, five waiting. Thomas signals the dash to fetch more bread.

The man sitting beside me settles his chin on my shoulder. His ear cups mine. His breath is a popcorn mist.

– Tom communes every time his teeth tear a crust.

His words scratch at my cheek like stubble.

– This is my body which is given for you. Take it.

– Leave my hand alone!

It's time to fast forward.

I shift to another seat. He follows.

Tom tucks in. Two or three oysters disappear in arrest — snip, snip, snip — as if by magic.

I switch rows, treading on toes. So does he.

Upscaling, downscaling, the Picture House pianist sways from side to side as she climbs then skelters down the keyboard. I return to the aisle. I spot an empty seat on the end of a row, hedged with gawpers on three sides. I take it. The scaling stops. I'm looking at a busy saloon bar in the 1920s. Some people are standing, some are seated. The camera is stationary. The action is scanty to say the least. A woman in a coat walks across the room. A man greets her. They turn away from the camera and leave the shot. The scene seems banal, unstaged.

– I'm not sure about this. It's like we're looking through a window, or at a security monitor. Does this shot belong here? Where's the story gone? I don't recognise anyone. Who are these people? Why the long take?

– It's the bar in the hotel. Tom's eating next door. The audience needs to become familiar with this space. A lot will happen here. The deep field is sown with hints. The police helmet. The cigar advert by the counter and the brolly stand. That woman in mourning. They're seedlings for scenes to come.

– It's too early. It doesn't work.

– You're right. Let's move it.

Champing on crust, give us this day, Tom imagines himself in the dining room of the Albemarle. It has a view of the clifftop bandstand. Last November the tuba was the only instrument proof against the wind. The vibrating columns of air released by finer gauges – trombones, trumpets, cornets, flutes – were dispersed before they reached the herbaceous border. Refugee fragments of billowing melody wafted over now and again. Fanny loved the effect. She told every guest she could that the martial pomp of yesteryear had been winnowed into jazz. And said it was high time too.

– Would you like to go over?

– I'd rather sit here with you.

Happy days, possibly their happiest. Did Otto get the message? Has he acted on it?

– I cannot send a wire Tom. There must be no trail.

– Quite right. And where could you send it anyway?

– To Marburg?

Tom will write in his journal tonight:

I am a fugitive. From whom, I know not (precisely, yet).

I come across these words at my desk in Sea Street, two minute's walk from where they were written. They were cited in court by the prosecution. Tom's lawyer jumped to his feet. He claimed maladaptation. He said the lines were inadmissible. The judge agreed.

Disembodied voices advance on the dining room.

– No one has seen him since lunchtime. He's a bloody liability.

– He won't be far. One can't disappear for long in a town this size.

– That's right. There's simply nowhere to hide.

– Where the hell has he gone? He's due on set first call.

– He'll be there.

– We can't move the story on without him. Find the sot now. Chullo, chullo. Bring him back here.

The door spits open. Into the dining room bursts a bear of a man, a hefty grizzler in a brown fur coat. Hirsute from nose to knee, he roars and bares four canine teeth shaking them like spears at Tom, myself, and the waiter. The dissolves are worthy of Eisenstein. We level our rifles and take aim. It's a stand-off. Loudmouth unbearable turns away, scanning the empty dining tables. Placing his paws on the ground, thrusting his fur buttocks high in the air, he wallops through the chairs.

– Dammit he's not here. Bloody well find him!

Cubs dart in and out and past the open door, making a show of urgency.

Thomas beckons to the waiter.

– It's the bear. But where's the key?

– Sir?

– Not on his shoulder. The key. Never mind.

– That's quite all right sir.

Two women follow the blustering beast through the door. The first flares tall, a living flame in a stab red dress. Her shadow, greyswathed, wilts beneath a sombrero that resembles a pizza dusted with ash.

– It's Bleede. And Dye.

– Sir?

His glass stalled halfway to his lips, Thomas cannot take his eyes off the new arrivals.

Bleede soothes the beast.

– Charles won't be far away. So sit, asseyez. Let's have something to eat while the boys round him up.

– He'd better not be smashed. We haven't got a budget for his bloody hangovers.

– I'm sure you're as hungry as we are.

The waiter stoops and whispers to Thomas.

– They are here to make a film sir. Adapting a story about the coast so I'm told. The tale of a second husband who turns out a brute, and the wife's revenge. That's the director, Mr Manning Hayes. The one in the hat is Daisy England, the leading lady. Charles Ashton is drinking our high street dry. The lady in red is responsible for the screenplay, Miss Lydia Hayward.

I jot down the names as Thomas upends his glass. Later I search for details online.

The Head of the Family, 1922. Five thousand five hundred feet and ninety minutes long. Silent. Based on a story by W W Jacobs. The other actors were Johnny Butt, Cynthia Murtagh and Moore Marriott. Three stills available. One festival screening. Contact the viewing service.

I cannot find a report anywhere of *The Head of the Family* being shown in Whitstable. There are no adverts for the film in the local paper. It was shot in the town, it was the talk of the town, but the high street cinemas didn't book it. Why's that? I find it odd. Was the film tainted? Too deeply associated with tonight's shame and scandal? Was it vinegared by Tom?

The bear grumbles an order for ribs and red wine. Soup arrives.

I step outside. From the courtyard balcony I watch Thomas tipping. He studies the threesome sipping. Onstage the band mess with stands and leads. The waiter plies the prattle with bottles, with chalices, and at last – bloody overdue don't you think? – a trio of pungent beef ribs.

Each one's hands went out to each one's feast.

Thomas in the corner. Nine empty, one raised, two waiting.

The bear is growling at the women, teeth bared, plying a glass with its paw. The rumble ends with a yap and a bestial grin. Bleede taps greyscale on the knee. The two women look up from their plates. They beam and titter. How ridiculous, they simply have no do they after all. Yatter yatter – then, a pause. The low growling resumes.

Darkness. An art nouveau surround appears on the screen. Two white trees frame an unlit void, their upper boughs interlaced. Young bears in suits cavort between them. A question bursts above their heads like a firework. The words sparkle.

IS FILM A THREAT TO CULTURE?

The frame fades. Scratch lightning flickers inaudibly across the vintage query.

A wash of light sweeps across two hundred upturned faces. At first the scene is a baffling canvas of geometric abstraction. Ten discs of white fabric on a dark ground. The circumference of two of these discs is broken, the largest with three bright lozenges, the other with one. The discs begin to look like cogs with wooden teeth. Two flexing radians extend into the smaller cog, six half-radians into the largest. Are they gearwheels? They begin to resemble clocks without numerals, with hands that flash. Oh, the teeth are chairs. Laughter follows as the audience realises it is looking down vertically on a nest of tables, its point of view that of a camera suspended in a skylight.

A small disc ricochets between the tables. It pings back and forth like the pixelated symbol for a ball in a half-remembered electronic console. The camera operator – seated at a monitor below the courtyard balcony – mouses in slowly to reveal the ball is a waiter supporting a large silver tray of glasses high above his shoulder.

– A collar button under a lens, thrown on the screen, may become a radiant planet.

– Give us a break Sergei. Unless you're going to lend a hand?

The waiter becomes a tonsured skull with a glittering shield beside him, a dancing figure of eight, leading first with one shoulder, then with the other, as he glides between the tables. A practised professional, he slips between cardio-bunnies fatburning to the band's first number, smiling indiscriminately. A man at work, an automaton. I order a steak. I order a salad. I order a soup. I'm not sure what I order. I've forgotten. I was on the brink of a yawning gulf between painting and the cinema, storytelling and gaming, music and dance. It was a chasm that would close and crush me if I fell into it. My scrotum tightened. I retreated from the edge of the balcony, giving up my view of the control unit, and turned to the window.

– We're having a lot of fun. We hope you are too.

The elderly singer's face is obscured by the dark bud of the microphone.

– I'm not sure what key that was at the beginning. Or keys. Bear with us, we're called Copperas and we do get better.

Perforated, choppy chords. A hand, strings, a hand again, a fiddler's bow, close-ups, song. The crowd knows the hook. Everyone joins in.

– He took a knife

– Twelve pieces

– He took hold

– Twelve pieces

– And deeeeeee vy did her

– He divided her

– And deeeeeee vy did her

Seated at his table, Thomas continues to tip and to suck. The denim thighs of dancers nether at his elbows. Floral butts bloom across the rim of the table. Di qua here, di la there, buffeting, boppling, down di gui, up di su, boomps a daisy.

Ten below.

Tom's wineglass shakes to the drum and bass barrage. It sidles across the ship's wheels, passing grinning sharks and shells as the floorboards flex beneath the hoofers. A backswung hand knocks the glass over. A dress ring tunks into the bowl. Ooooh I'm sorry.

Fanny's blood sops into the cushions.

A retroteen in a leather blouse brays at the spillage. She points out the mishap to a young companion. The waiter is unable to get through the crush of dancers to help. The lad crumples a crisp packet. He lobs it at Thomas.

– You need to finish up mate. You're in the way there.

– Don't know what oysters munch on dooyer? If yer did yer wouldn't.

– Hwahwhawhahooa!

– Fred the Shed! Ow's yer evening been mate?

The glass rolls from the table and shatters on the floor. The bottle follows too as a dancer, dodging shards, rocks it over. People step away, others rubberneck. Root patterns and neck tatts bloom below the band. The musicians glance at each other and shrug. They play on as the audience turns away.

– He took a knife

Tom is on his feet. He can't see me from inside. It's dark out here. He bangs on the window. He tries to raise the lower sash, squat-thrusting against the frame. The window resists. It won't open. He knocks a potted cactus to the floor. The container smashes. Mr Manning Hayes, Daisy England and Lydia Hayward of Artistic Pictures turn towards the disturbance. They see a solitary diner having a panic attack at the far end of the room – shell shock perhaps? They don't get up to help him. That's the waiter's job. Where is he? The crowd bottlenecks at the door. I can't get in.

Tom is rescued by the banter of the band.

– We're over here.

– Turn around bright eyes.

– Let him alone you don't know where he's bin.

– D'yer know y'all look minging from behind?

Tom is at the window, head in his hands. Then hunger was more powerful than sorrow. He returns to the table.

– Right you lot, any requests?

– Secondhand!

– Words sound like a knife?

– Oright. That'll do nicely.

A vague suspicion of everyone and everything filled my mind. Just for a moment I had a premonition of approaching evil.

Three beats into the bass solo the judge rapped the block with his gavel. The hall fell silent. The band pounded mutely. Modern dance lacks grace when the music can't be heard. Most moves suggest a state of madness. A bewildered man eats the remains of a meal beside a silenced band that is playing to a crowd in spasm.

The beauty of silence. Active looking. The pantomimic art.

A voice from the darkness says a fuse has blown in the projection room.

The Picture House pianist tolls a mid range note with one finger as she rummages for a handkerchief. She sneezes loudly. Twice.

The audience catcalls.

– Hump to the rescue!

– We should have gone to the multiplex.

– You wouldn't be told.

In the Duke the next morning, mothers chat over coffee. Their children run around the tables and climb on and off the stage.

– Sound went at the flicks last night. Again. Don't jump off there Maisie, you'll fall and hurt yerself.

– So I heard. Refund?

– But mu-um. I want to.

– Trip switch blew like a bottle smashing. Yeah. An don't come crying to me when you do.

New voices, new possibilities, always more. Is that the click of billiard balls? Sir John Dimsdale organised tournaments here. The table drew a better class of customer to the hotel. Blue chalk appears on my fingers. I wipe it off.

Maisie looks towards her mother, who is no longer watching. She bends her knees then springs into the air, flinging her arms wide like wings. An angel, a seagull, defiant. As she lands, she slips. Her left knee drives into her chin. Her shriek shatters the tiara of glass flowers in the skylight above our heads.

I flinch as silicate shards, sharp as arrows, clatter and gouge into the tabletops. Startled, Tom rises from his seat by the window. Mum looks over her shoulder.

– There. I told you. Come here you silly girl.

The glass holds.

Tom lips the last shell, slurping vinegar. He chews the pallid flesh in gourmandising slow motion before dabbing his grin with a napkin. The band finish their song.

– Thank you. Thank you. We're back after shampers.

Whooping, claps and stamping, well-heeled Kentish fire banked in lavish trainers. Red-faced men rush to the bar. They raise fingers, eyebrows and twenty pound notes to the alespinners. The Duke's till-feeding troupe of barkeeps stoops and sells, bending then vending – ooze necks? – with scarcely a word.

In the corner Tom fingers the ice beneath the husks. He smears his forehead with melt. He's in a sanatorium in Lausanne. Roger Vittoz is shelving Tom's brow with the flanks of his hands. The doctor measures the thought waves of his patients daily. The cool edges of his palms log length. They capture cadence. They index intensity.

– I will train you in brain control Thomas. This will overcome the torpor and mental wandering that you report. Your pulsation should be regular, between 35 and 100 beats a minute. We will help you achieve this.

– Help me doctor. Please.

Unbuckling his wristwatch, Vittoz studies Tom's temple.

– Ideas should be ruled by reason and judgement. Ideas should be subject to your will. I will help you to make your thoughts and your actions voluntary. First I will teach you elimination of thought. You will learn how to deconcentrate, how to detach from the eruption of words. To detach from the eruption. To detach. With time there will be a growth in calmness, control, and decision. Every day I will check the rhythm you have achieved. Once you have learnt how to deconcentrate, Thomas, I will help you to concentrate again with a new precision.

– You are a poet, Vittoz. You are going to write me. To rewrite me. You're a classicist. You're a critic. You're the editor I've dreamed about. I do so need this.

– Relax, Thomas. Imagine the figure eight. Approach the curve of the figure and follow it round, the full double undulation. Let it carry you.

– You will help me to manage and order my experiences. You are going to rebalance my sensibility. Vittoz, you are tradition! Will you lay my Donne to rest?

– Explain that to me.

– In the years leading up to the war, the war which has not yet ended, Donne had thoughts and experiences that were profound and intense. He was unable to control them. As a poet Donne failed to impose order.

– The war is over, Thomas. It ended in nineteen eighteen.

– Since Donne emotion and intelligence have lived under separate rooves. Pound me into shape Vittoz. Help me put them back together.

– I'm here to cure your aboulie, Thomas. It's not my job to patch up poetry.

– You must take care not to rub out science. Leave me my common sense. I don't want to end up naked, far from tradition, seeing only nakedness. Don't leave me like Billy-no-mates Blake. Bodybuild my sensibility, Vittoz, help me connect. Hey doc can you make me into Baudelaire? What a poet! He was able to study his own suffering.

– Twice four is? Undulate. Follow it.

– Please God I don't end up a Milton or a Browning. That's a risk I'll have to take. Hey ho, let's go. Cut off the stale crusts of opinion, doc. Uncloud me. Help me to fight the deterioration of language.

– One step at a time, Thomas.

Vittoz cups Tom's forehead with his hands.

– This is it doc, the coronation of a poet.

– Let that thought go.

The clink of Fanny's bracelet by his eyes.

– You brokedick excuse for a man!

Someone is shouting in the corridor of the hotel. Security are on to it.

– Leave me alone you fucker. Why don't you chuck her out?

– This way sir.

– She follows me everywhere. Why don't you bar her? Give me some space you bitch! Everywhere, she follows me everyfuckingwhere.

– You're leaving, mate. Now.

Strange utterances, horrible pronouncements, accents of anger, words of suffering, voices shrill and faint, and beating hands.

Soon after there is an explosion.

It is laughter, from the circle around the director. In extreme close up, the camera pans across the elasticating lips of the women, teething wide in deferential glee. Winefog condenses on the lens as they hoot in unison.

– You sure about this?

The shot tilts downwards. Two hundred faces in the kinema audience are mopped with a giant handkerchief. The cloth plunges the auditorium into darkness before lifting away to reveal the empty stage of the Duke. The spotlights in the backdrop have been rearranged to say

INTERLUDE: IN A BAR

Matches flare, flints spit, tips glow and blaze. Here, far from the day, there is no sense of time passing.

– Here he comes.

– I'll do the honours.

As Thomas enters the crowded saloon a portly man, slickhaired in a worn suit and round eyeglasses, steps forward to greet him.

– Wood, pleasedtermeetcha. I own the garage across the way. Come wash your neck with us, why don't you?

There is a scab on his chin. A moth tie nips at his greying throat. Pan down to the extended hand. The buttons that bridle his paunch don't match. The cuff is frayed; there's no watch. A chain runs from a belt clip to his pocket.

– Stern. Thankyou. Here for the one night, that's all. On my way to Cliftonville.

They have heard he's a banker. An artisan of the Square mile. Will trade perk up at all this year? Sbeen a battering, what? How long before Blighty is back on her feet? Any advice for local traders?

– Get the man another gin.

– Tip us the sling on anything you can, Stern. We'd be very grateful.

In Wood's opinion — he's looked into it thorough — coal is the best opportunity for the town.

– We fetch lump in through the harbour, from Newcastle, thousands of tons of black diamonds every year. Brown, our merchant, distributes around the county by road and by rail. Now that Kent has mines, it's flowing the other way too. Coal in, coal out, the union will soon be calling for canaries down on the quay. Incoming loads are often sold on. Sometimes the men have to refill the colliers with the same lump they lifted out. They joke about leaving the cargoes on board and waving the skipper on. They don't understand markets.

– Oh they of little faith.

– It won't be long before we have more coal here than we need, Mr Stern. The tooter the sweeter, I say. Brown wins hands down either way and the town will prosper with him, whatever our moaners say about the trucks. Never mind the noise, or the dust, the mineowners are sinking shafts into our future. The downside is trade unions and Bolsheviks breed in the pits. Do all they can to disrupt the trade. But we will deal with that Mr Stern. Coal for London, that's our future.

– Well put Woods.

– He'll put your shirt on it.

– Hahahahahaaaa.

– Gentlemen, I don't know Whitstable but I do know London. Your capital is adequately supplied with cheap coal. You may have to export yours. Give it some consideration. If the tunnel is a success, Paris will soon be a nearer neighbour than Newcastle.

– The tunnel is outlandish, Mr Stern, an ill-conceived swindle. Why would anyone who cares about England run a burrow under our moat? A rat run for the French, that's what it is. An invitation to the Hun. It must not happen. It will not. The usurers behind Sir Arthur Fell are not welcome in Kent.

– English coal for English hearths, that's the business.

– The franc won't stand fast, it never has. The cockney pound Stern, you can depend on that.

– How certain is it that coal from Kent will always pass this way? Hasn't Dover the larger harbour? Isn't the pier at Richborough closer to the collieries?

– Richborough's job is done. That port was built to get tanks and shells to Tommies in the line, and that alone. The war's over, nobody lives there, there's no call for it now. Dover's a threat, agreed. We must keep the trade here. Can you hear them out in the Cross tonight? They may be fools but they're our fools. The boatyards are done for. The government is going to abolish guaranteed prices for food supplies. Farmers aren't planting, and when they do they'll mechanise. Without work our men may desert the flag. By Christmas, Stern, there could be Soviets up and down the estuary.

– They're not reds, Wood. Most of the families out there are local, the men are decent types. We must do something for them don't you think?

– Isn't that why we set them on the sea wall?

– The government should help. The minister is a tightfisted shirker.

– If the state hires these men, Twigger will say private enterprise isn't needed any more.

– Except to cough up taxes. Red squandermania, that's their plan.

– Twigger drips with class hatred.

– The rhythm of regular work would restore their belief in us.

– I have talked with Lieutenant Colonel Sims. He says socialists understand the bigger picture but they intend to change it. He says they are discovering their potential.

– Which is?

– 'The capacity to change the course of history itself.'

– Good God man. Where does that leave us?

Tom laughs.

– Their potential is very well disguised. Listen. They have the capacity to chant but no knowledge of music.

Tom conducts the outdoor singing as a window cleaner would, arcing an imaginary cloth across an unseen pane of glass.

– True indeed.

– They will vote without reason. The massenmensch will bawl and hustle and smash against the Hyde Park railings.

Tom spins a finger by his forehead. He tongue bursts from his mouth. He pumps it sloppily between his lips.

– He's half slewed.

– Massenwhat in Hyde Park?

– Bubbed.

– He's bubbed but he's right.

Tom holds his nose. Below the pinch, his lips purse disgust.

– There are cheese mites in the national cheese.

– Indeed, indeed there are.

– Does your mum know you're out?

– Action Francaise leads the way. Camelots du Roi to the rescue!

– The frogs and King Arthur? What kind of a banker are you?

A clerical collar appears round Tom's neck. In wonderment they became pale. Tom genuflects. He clasps his hands.

– Help us to strengthen the values we hold in common. Family. Honesty. Faith. A settled way of life upon the land.

– Amen to that.

– He's Gilbert the filbert, the colonel of the nuts!

As Aiken pointed out, Tom was capable of real buffoonery.

Another gabster bellies through the fumes. I note the gleaming ribbon on his boater, lapis lazuli below the tarstained chandelier, The bowl of his pipe has a silver girdle.

– Davey. The draper. Pleased to.

– Stern. How do.

– Tell our guest how you see the future of the town.

– Fires and floods. Arsonists and inundations. No boatyard left to build an ark

– Hahaaarha.

– Seriously, man. Stopper the guff.

– The next Brighton, that's what Whitstable could be. A coastal resort of distinction. Tankerton is half way there, setting the pace. We have to clear the waterfront and build more hotels.

– Would anyone come? This is a working town. I mean, well it used to be.

– A road along the coast would help. The motor car is the future, that's as clear as day. The purchase price of vehicles will tumble as more are made. Their mechanisms will become more dependable. I do believe there will be motoring for the masses before long. And when that happens, my friends, we must make sure that every signpost points to Whitstable.

– The future is Ford?

– I know it sounds cranky, Mr Stern, but it's quite possible that the children of the mob outside will learn how to drive. Just think of it. Motor cars for us, motor cars as well as motor cycles for the labouring class. A nation motoring to its shoreline to paddle and to lodge and scoff every weekend. For our town to prosper, we must plan for that.

Tom folds his arms and strokes his chin.

– You'd like Whitstable to be Long Island? Let's think it through. First, if he lives in a boarding house or a tenement, where does a man put his automobile? Second, these incoming vehicles, where will you store them?

– We'll build more garages, Mr Stern. Adapt the barns and the stables, drain a few fields if we have to. We'll need you, the banks, to start lending again.

– You'll need more roads, and bigger roads too. The state will take your fields for highways. Your front gardens as well, to broaden rural lanes. Bridges and tunnels will be needed to connect them. Kent will become a tangle of tarmacadam and concrete. Would you motor to see that? And if you did, would you stay? Every destination will be obliterated by a route to somewhere else. What charm would Whitstable retain? Coast, farmland and community will disappear so motor cars can billet here on concrete beds.

– Sunny side up with you tonight isn't it?

– Your doors will open on to a labyrinth of accidents and noise. Your civilisation will decay. You'll become a motorised, wandering absence of culture. Cars are replacing horses, gramophones are displacing musicians, theatres are being deposed by cinemas. They too will be degraded in their turn.

– This is not America, Mr Stern.

– Aeroplanes will circle overhead with nowhere to land. The garden of Kent will fill with strangers. The churches will stand empty. Is that what you want?

– You're laying it on a bit thick.

– Tosh. We'll make it work, you'll see.

– I may exaggerate. I've no knowledge of the local situation.

– Fair enough old man.

– The internal combustion engine flattens the rhythm of life. It is corrupting the rhythm of poetry.

– No doubt. Quite so.

– Words to heed and ponderate.

– Drink?

– That's kind of you. Gentlemen, I'm far from home. I'm a Yankee Doodle living in Albion, a resident alien. Yet I believe that men, most men, should worship, work and marry as close to their place of birth as possible. That is the only way to preserve what really matters.

– Which is? Out with it, Stern.

– He means England.

– No. What really matters is the mind of Europe.

– Mind of Europe?

– No boodle in that.

– No jobs for the men outside either.

And late into the night they studied the workers' welfare.

Not far from where Tom stood I come across an old advertisement, framed and displayed beside the bar.

> *When you buy a Cigar see that it is of a distinctive Brand. There's a reputation behind the name. Buy a CRITERION.*

– How I tired of that word.

– It was seventeen years of your life.

And chosen by Fanny. I wanted to call it the *London Review*.

> THE CRITERION aims at the maintenance of international standards. In the belief that the intellectual life of Europe, like its economic life, depends upon communication and exchange, it will present in translation writings of foreign men of letters, whose work should be better known in England.

> *Manufactured from the choicest leaf. Samples of 5 for 3/-. In cedar*

wood boxes of 25, 50 and 100. Exact size of Imperial No 2.

THE CRITERION aims also at the constant revision of the critical opinions of literature.

– Is our society dissembled round anything more termagent than conger eels of banks, assurance chimpanzees and outdustries?

– It has been a pleasure meeting you, Mr Stern.

– I'll second that chum.

– And I must be off.

– Has it any tealeafs more essenced in oil than tealeaf in divided ends?

Exact size of Imperial No.3. Uniform in quality. Moderate in price. All high class tobacconists and stores.

– Do you require a match sir?

The saloon has filled with flabby-faced men, sharpers who did well from the war, a wife or two and tipsy cacklers. Smoke battles with scent in the phantosmia I now inhabit with Tom.

Scent triumphs, briefly. We find ourselves standing in a mob of ballers and creepers, mobility scooter hotshoes and bakes with tatts, oddjob entrepreneurs and penniless musos. They yell updates at each other through a chemical mist of sham sniff and discount deodorant.

– Bought the new wheels din I.

– Got those tickets.

– So I told him.

– Showed her the door.

– Don't let meee be lonely. Ternight.

At the rear of the building the musicians are back on the stage.

Thomas scorches by the fire. I switch my seat to get a better view.

He's a nobody to the people here, now as then. The risk of recognition is sub-zero tonight. Exposure and arrest are no more likely than requests for selfies and autographs. It's chillax time.

Outside in the Cross, strikers, socialists and their families rally to the streetlamp. Flapping red nosewipes they sing at the top of their voices, blowing as one. Cloth caps, straw hats and headscarves tilt towards the stars. With a martial hymn they block the Duke's rocksonic cannonade.

– Fight the good lonesome tonight fight with all miss me tonight might sorry we strength and drifted apart does your right.

A familiar voice, as powerful as fifty voices of other men.

– Nationalise the railways!

Polyphony, a charming of the senses, disabling thought.

– Run the straight kiss you called seek chairs before us lies.

A big-voiced singer who sounds like a calf. The others howl around him like dogs.

A sty of contentment.

One can't make out a word they are saying. It's impossible.

So a striker mounts the box cart to shout an intertitle:

MAKE THE BANKERS PAY!

Through a side window on to Harbour Street Thomas sees two men sharing a butt. Each has a medal pinned to an empty sleeve.

Thomas puts his book down on the mantelpiece. He places his glass beside it and looks over to me. I nod. Yes, I'll keep an eye on them.

He steps out on to the pavement.

The veterans perk up.

– Tanner for two workless soldiers, sir?

– We're no good for the dredging, or for the building trade.

– Or we wouldn't be asking yer.

There is shouting from the rally under the streetlamp. Tenpence an hour! Pay the fair rate! Stragglers hurry towards the junction. The three men by the porch look towards the meeting.

– I fought for my country in the war. I have no house to return to. No graft or gelt was waiting for me.

– We kip in a bell tent, sir, in a field in Tankerton. With my wife and two other men in the same unfortunate state. We cook in a bucket..

I know that the wife of the taller squatter is pregnant. Does he? The child will die under mildewed canvas within the year. Soon after, police officers arrive with hatchets and spades. The tent is torn down. That man and his wife are separated. They are placed in the Union, the workhouse at Blean.

– I tried to enlist. They would not let me serve.

– Lucky bugger. Might yer help out two flatmen who did?

Thomas takes a few steps towards the meeting. The speaker's words elbow their way through the crowd towards him.

– When we speak out, they try and move us on. I say the people of this town have met here at the Cross for decades. The Liberals rally here. We don't object. The employers gather here. We don't object. The Salvation Army is always here, there's many of us glad they are. But when Labour meets at the Cross they call it an obstruction. Brothers, we are not an obstruction. We are clearing the way to socialism.

– Hisrightfairratehurrahhhlapclapap.

The two troopers flank the banker.

– Cadbury, Rowntree, farsighted guvnors, honourable men, they know fair wages are the true economy. Yet here in Whitstable, after tough grind, after the rent collectors squeeze us, we have what, a paltry seventeen shillings left to feed our families and keep the kiddies warm. In Canterbury and in Faversham men like us get a fair rate for the work. Tuppence more an hour. Why is our sweat unrewarded? We dine out on the smells from the Butcher's kitchen. For victory in mud and blood, we have been paid with ashes, with fruit from the Dead Sea. Over there officers with pensions, merchants, men whose pockets jingle with our rent are carousing with councillors who keep ours empty. They are standing together against us. We must stand together against them. Miners. Railwaymen. Seamen. Men in work, men without work, our wives too. We must to battle again as we did when comrades in arms.

Snotters wave, caps and hats whirl.

– Srite. Hisrightobattlagin. Comraylapapapclap!

The cheers of the crowd engulf the orator's words.

Years later I discussed the speech with the sister of the man who gave it.

– Matthew worked in the timberyard. His voice was like a maul driving wedges into the trunk of the town, riving the people that sat pretty from people like us. Fairness. *Thwack!* Nationalise. *Thwack!* Tax. *Thwack!* His words cracked the way we'd looked at things wide open. In the saloon of the Duke they were in it for themselves we all knew that. Out there we had to stand up for us selves. We so many, crowding the way. Folk pushed in so tight to hear him I could hardly take my breath. We knocked they wedges deeper with our claps and cheers, splitting a different future, ours, from their past. He said we should build a fleet of barges and ambush the steamers. We should board the liners and set sail for socialism. My brother he launched a ship of dreams along the high street. It only lasted half an hour. The town, to me it never looked the same again.

The tallest rough sleeper nods to his pal, placing himself between Thomas and the protest. Slowly, he shuffles backwards until his shoulderblades prod the banker's chest. Tom takes two steps back. The shuffle resumes. As Tom withdraws a second time he is shoved into the hotel porch. The shorter veteran pins him against the cold tiles with his only forearm. The other takes two more steps to the rear, masking the raid from passers by.

My view of what happens next is obscured.

– An if yer aven't a tanner, ten bob will do.

Shorty's reek scythes up at Tom's beak.

– Make it a quid. At least.

They box him in more tightly.

– Now, feller. Tootderfuckingsweet let's have it.

Tom complies. The men walk off in opposing directions, one towards the Cross, joining the crowd, the other towards the harbour, flitting up an alley.

As Tom comes back into the saloon, the peal of the orator enters with him.

– They have land. They have stocks. They have pensions. Pensions, stock and land. What do we have? Poverty. A poverty that is preventable. A poverty not prevented. We have been paid with eviction notices. We should be paid to build ourselves new homes.

– hoooraaaaaaaahurahahaaaaaah

The door swings shut, muting the cheers.

– Next up he'll demand land to build on.

– Free bricks an best timber too.

– They help themselves to those already.

– That man, he has the look of an assassin.

I turn but not quickly enough to spot the speaker. It's impossible to tell which of the huddle the laughter rewards. Was she referring to the soapbox socialist? Can she see him from there? Tom is returning to the fireplace, pocketing his purse. On his face there is a look of desolation. The words may not have been directed at him.

– What were you thinking at that moment? War brutalises men? That you should be more cautious on the street? Or had Fanny come to mind, burning her way through your current account?

– That's very unfair. No, it was Verdy. Jean Verdenal. We shared a pension in Paris, the bis rue St Jacques, more than ten years ago.

– Arms full of lilac in the Luxembourg Gardens?

– No. Corpsing in the brine of the bloody Dardanelle.

Look. A bloater, face down in the ebb tide.

What strange fish has made his meal upon thee?

The bank issued a memorial volume, a photographic mausoleum for the fallen. Leaders without equal, managers middling, ranks of clerks incalculable. Those who served and did not return to the counter.

– A subscription agent brought a sample to the office in King William Street. It was filled with images of tense but smiling men, three to four on a page. Professional portraits, oval likenesses, cheaper snaps. Some were vaguely familiar, I thought. Except here, the eyes of Jean, and there, his brow. Limbs scattered across the leaves. More than once his mouth, his youthful radiance.

In the entrance hall in Lombard Street, at the foot of the main stairway, there is a permanent monument to the dead. Corpses tallied on a stone ledger, remembrance in an enduring form. It was unveiled by the chairman, Sir Richard Vassar-Smith, in February 1921. Call of King and country. Path of duty and self sacrifice. Six hundred and eighty six names are inscribed on black marble. Half a dozen fell beside Verdy at Gallipoli. In November, Thomas did not share the silence of the clerks. He was at the Albemarle in Cliftonville.

– Let those who come after see to it that their names are not forgotten.

The City of London excels at forgetting. The return on the respect invested in the monument failed to justify the floorspace. A gloomy fossil, the ageing headstone became an eyesore in the Square Mile's bigged up and banged atrium of bulletproof glass. Let them be remembered some other time, in some other place. I tracked the displaced slabs to a storage branch in Bristol where I paid my last respects.

In the far corner of the saloon two women are sharing one glass of wine. I spot the deft top-up beneath the table, a splash of handbag vodka.

So does Tom. Reunited with his gin, he has recovered from the ambush. Writing is no longer an option tonight. McDollar will have to wait.

His thoughts, thoughts which are felt, thoughts which lack precision but smell like roses, his thoughts, if such they are, are turning to the hotel trot-about in blue, to the dancer in the window across the street, to perfume wafting from a flaming dress.

Will you stay on the scent with me, I wonder. Is Tom's story worth your candle?

Just then a she-wolf of a woman showed herself. She seemed to carry every craving in her leanness. She has left Manning howling alone at his table. When she has fed, she's hungrier than ever. Her eyes surpass the splendour of the stars.

She heads towards Thomas, gazed on like a comet, savouring the school of eyes that her passage nets.

– Mr Stern, is it not? I looked up your name in the register. Welcome. I'm so pleased to meet a fellow writer here.

She has a few years on him. He knows her accent is from the north. Yorkshire?

– It is. For an American you have a good ear. Mr Conan, on reception, tells me you're a banker. But I know your secret.

Her whisper sears his ear.

– The skull beneath the skin.

Tom gasps. He gags on her perfume. He cannot breathe. He hears police whistles. Rozzers rush at him with handcuffs. She pokes him, playfully, in the midriff.

– The last twist of the knife.

The nabbers slam the door to his cell. The hangman curls a noose.

– I know your work Mr Stern. Don't look so surprised. The Egoist? The Dial? You are a critic and a poet as well as a banker. Hayward. Lydia. Scriptwriter. Plots, lists of shots and title cards for the flickers. We are making part of a film here in the town, Head of the Family, from a short story by W W Jacobs.

She picks up Thomas's book, riffling through the cut pages.

– I've heard about this. How tremendous that you have a copy. May I?

She moves toward a standing lamp, reading from a page. Tom blinks and bobsleighs around a Swiss figure of eight, lunging for its double undulation. The switchback slows at a terrace café beside a lake that drains into the Duke.

> Her tall slender form, outlined against the bright light; the vivid sense of slumbering fire that seemed to find expression only in those wonderful tawny eyes of hers, remarkable eyes, different from any other woman's that I have ever known; the intense power of stillness she possessed, which nevertheless conveyed the impression of a wild untamed spirit in an exquisitely civilised body – all these things are burnt into my memory. I shall never forget them.

Miss Hayward returns to Tom's side.

– Breathtaking.

– It is so good I wish I had never read it.

– A hat rack, two bags full. Merveilleux.

– I haven't got that far.

It doesn't take long. Soon it's this film and that film, the cowboy Tom Mix and can the Inferno, with darkness visible and black light, ever be made for the screen. Have you heard the whispers about sound, and the pipedream of colour?

A tour group of Chinese students enters the bar, lengthening like a fence across the room then folding. Women shenme shihou keyi jiandao Slawson zhuren? Straws, rice straws, in the rising wind from the east. Another future shimmers on the town's horizon. I edge around its rucksack perimeter until I am back in earshot.

– Chaplin owes a debt to the liturgy, to the church.

– His biggest debt is to a woman, Tom. He stole gestures and expressions, complete routines as well, from Mabel Normand. Don't you know that? She was a director at Keystone well before Charlie blew in. Were the gags less funny when she did them?

– I've not heard this before. Mabel Normand, I say. Are you sure?

– Manning and I met Charlie in London recently, up at the Savoy. He was miffed when I mentioned her. Slapped the back of his own hand and served me up that smile. Still, thief or not, the man's a genius. There's a magnificent scene in his latest, *The Idle Class*. Have you seen it?

– Why yes. Only yesterday.

– A wife walks out on her husband, he's a hopeless drunk. Filmed from behind, the man appears to be sobbing uncontrollably. Then he turns round. There are no tears at all. The souse is rattling a cocktail shaker, fixing a drink. It was a hoot.

– It certainly was. Ha! I mean hoot!

It was a mass, he thinks. Suffering and a proffered sip.

– It reminded me of daddy.

– I'm sorry to hear that.

I can smell his insincerity. She's nearer. She's no excuse.

A young woman with a pushchair trolleys through the sportswear, grating ankles, shoving at shanks. Wotchit babe. Whoah! I slide towards a new vantage point. A guy in a brown hoodie barges past. I'm shunted into a bored couple. Some minor spillage. They turn and glare. I apologise. Lydia is speaking.

– A second marriage to a bullying husband. The wife hires a young man to pose as her long lost son and defend her. There's romance, of course, and humour. Charles Ashton, he's in it. You must have heard of him? And Johnny Bett. Johnny and I have worked together before. Three Men in a Boat? You must know it. Of course you do. Manning is directing. We'll be shooting on the beach tomorrow. Do come and join us, Tom. Please.

– I might, Miss Hayward.

– I say you must, Mr Stern.

– Film is entertaining, Lydia. I concede that. I thought it was a fad at first, canned drama. I've yet to be convinced that it's an art. Rapid action to incessant music. It has a future I suppose but it will never match live performance. Think of Marie Lloyd. Her banter with the audience in a music hall marries the stage to the stalls. Tiers of tears and laughter, full-throated joyous singing in which anyone can join. Can the pratslaps of dumb mannequins, can hokey in a dim room, ever match that?

– How deliciously incestuous, Thomas. Lloyds seduced by Marie Lloyd.

– Ha. Good shot.

– Bankers lured to their doom by the Siren of the East End. And don't dilly dally on the way.

Lydia winks. Tom blushes.

– Oh I, the, er, Ballet Russe too. In a performance a relationship is created…

She laughs at him.

– I'm teasing Thomas. I do understand you but like most people I simply love the cinema. At first I wanted to be an actress. I modelled myself on Mabel Normand for the audition. For days and days I practised that peculiar way she looks at the camera when she's confused.

Lydia's eyebrows rise, trailed by the tip of her nose and a dawdling lip.

– I spent hours in front of a glass. I was second rate.

– Fanny tried too. Fanny my, er, wife. With the same result.

– For every one that's hired, a thousand are turned away. That's how it is. Undeterred, I wrote a novel about a milkmaid who becomes a movie star. It was rejected. Everywhere I sent it. Unanimously. There's no woman worth printing, that's what publishers think. Between bedcovers not bookcovers, that's where the chaps want us. What am I for, I used to ask myself. There's so little time. My life was grey. Then right out of the blue, I mean the grey, obviously, Artistic Films asked me to adapt a story. And here I am, in Hollywood on Thames, hobnobbing with an American poet.

– So little time. I feel that too.

– What would you choose as a profession, if you consulted your inclination only? Do tell me.

– You'll laugh.

– Go on.

– I've always had a secret hankering to be a detective!

Each mirrors the other's laughter.

Leaning in close, Lydia fingers the back of his hand.

– Thomas. May I borrow your book for an hour?

– Of course you may.

– I could return it a little later. To your room if you like?

– Ah. I don't think that would be

– Do tell me about Mrs Stern. Where is she tonight?

A dangling foot. Shoe fallen to the floor.

– In London. Exactly where I really couldn't say.

– You lead separate lives?

Tom sings. The camera retreats each time he makes a step towards it.

When first I met Fanny
I fell head over heels
We were both to be writers
And our love was real.

When last I saw Fanny
Twere heels over head
There were sharp words between us
And now she is dead.

He will describe the encounter with Lydia to the sergeant tomorrow.

– She was prying into my private life. She was persistent. She was intrusive.

– We're not here to discuss Miss Hayward's bruises.

– I had been drinking.

– None of this is pertinent.

– She wouldn't let me alone. It was only a push.

AGON

At the far end of the bar, two men shunt a heavy table against the front door of the hotel. They place another upside down on top of it. Hefty objects are stacked between the raised legs: a hatstand, a scuttle full of coal, two wooden barrels. The preserved lower leg of an elephant lends cinematic weight to the barricade. As it has been hollowed out to serve as an umbrella bin, the director reminds the actors to flex and grimace as they lift it.

A bear lumbers into the rear of the saloon from the dining room. By the time he reaches the bar Hayes has shrunk into a young cub with a rattan cane under one arm and a Soviet cap on his head.

– We've met before.

– Open the music archive. Find a Russian fiddle.

– Theft of gold from Spain?

Ms Hayward steps away from Tom, turning her back on her boss.

– Lydia!

He bellows. It's a command performance. The cub has vanished.

Chat-ups go on hold. Bants cease. Every head is turned to Hayes with one exception, a barfly extending an anecdote like a teenager stretching gum.

– In Bratislava we were, the end of me mate's stag, it's still a pound a pint in Bratislava, they drink a kind of pilsners there, that will do me nicely I thought, and as we only paid ninety four quid for the flight and the hostel, we had a great time, like you do. Then just as we're getting on the plane back, a bit the worse for wear, what we went for weren't it, I could see the security up front in first class, I didn't think nothing much of it really, first knocking anyways, karaoke nobodies get bodyguards these days, not real musos any of them are they, then I saw him, I thought I know who that is, wow I said you'll never guess, I said to my mate do you know who that is, it's only Dylan ain't it. Bleedin' Bob Dylan on the same bleedin' plane as us. Do what he said to me. Dylan I says, you deaf, blowin' in the wind with us to Gatwick, he started paying attention then, so I says to the security, nice bloke he was, from Chicago, he told me back in the day he used to work all the big venues, huge bloke he was, seen all the world class bands when they were still up and coming, he spent proper time with them you know, poolside an that, I said any chance do you think, and he said there might be maybe later, wow I thought, me luck's in, choccy eggs at Christmas, and then the curtain opened again and I saw it wasn't Bob after all so anyway...

Hayes interrupts.

– God almighty, it's like sharing a migraine listening to that. What sin are you all paying for? Jazz plates, Lydia. For the gramophone. Chollo, chollo. Hurry up Hayward. It's time to wake these antiques up.

A snouty trumpet sniggers ragtime through the smoky saloon.

– Show us yer moves, gowon.

Acceding to the request from the bar Hayes dances the Grizzly Bear, a Broadway prance. He stomps into the centre of the room with ungainly steps, arms dangling, moobs and shirt studs plunging left then right to the bumping double bass. The sportswear cheers. Lydia returns to Tom.

– You say very little about yourself.

Tom raises his hands in mock alarm.

– I'll confess to murder if you promise not to tell.

– You are very evasive, Thomas. You duck every question. I believe I could write a script based on your secrets.

– I write, Miss Hayward. That means I spend most of my life at a desk.

I asked him later why he was so reticent.

– I knew nothing about her. We had only just met. And I thought, imagine that, a two-reeler about myself and Fanny. How appalling.

And so it was.

> The Dark Side of Genius. An American Predator (*St Louis Standard*)
>
> L'Horreur! L'Horreur! Le poète comme victim deux fois (*Tribune de Paris*)
>
> How Fanny Stern was mugged by medics (*Wombmen's Review*)

Hayes bows and heads back to the bar. Lydia shouts over the applause.

– I want to write another novel, Thomas, and I need a first rate idea. As a woman I can't fritter time away on something half-baked. It simply won't get looked at. The story of a modern-day American in London with a British wife could be just the ticket. She says tomato, he says potato, castrato, vibrato you know the kind of thing. He's a banker by day but a poet when the moon blooms. Just like a werewolf! That would be his secret. His wife must never find out. At night he breaks into libraries and bookshops to gorge on poetry, but the verses must always be the very best. Travelling for the bank he risks capture in exotic cities, forcing an entry into mosques and palaces and garrets to satisfy his craving. Oh Tom it could be a romance and a comedy and gothic and highbrow too. Will you help me? Can I meet Mrs Stern?

– It's a very amusing idea.

– Thomas! You too? Opposed to the Feminine in Literature?

The windows of the hotel crimson. This would never have happened at the Albemarle, Tom thinks. Lydia squints through lettering in the sandblast.

– How delightful. More starvelings rising from their slumber. Come on, let's go looksee.

She pulls him to a side door. As he is led outside, Tom places a hand on his wallet. A trade union banner seals the top of the street like the curtain of a theatre, promising drama while delaying it.

– This is Dante in our time, Tom. Can you see it? A banner that, as it wheels about, races on. Behind the banner trails so long a file of people.

– Yes Lydia, I do see it. That's a description of the lost.

– Don't spoil it for me. If the class war continues I'm going to buy a red ribbon like that for my typewriter. Isn't it glorious! Why isn't anyone making films about this – the postwar crusade of our picturesque proletariat?

Tom is thinking what would be the point? Hope doesn't come from people who march in step. But he turns to her and says:

– Forget the werewolf Lydia. This is the story you're looking for.

Ninety years later, I join them on the street.

What did Tom see?

A shabbily dressed mass, dolts bawling beneath a blanket of caps and cheap straw hats. Torchlight red on sweaty faces. Crutches, scrawled placards, muddy skirts and scraps of uniform. Lamplit flags lethargic, defiant stares.

The menacing glint of medals on greatcoats. Men trained in the use of battlefield knives. Danger.

I watch as a tramp in a bowler bandylegs along Harbour Street waving a black flag. I know that it's red. Frame by frame, I restore the anger, paintbrush in hand. Behind its glow, a Charlot troupe, mechanised. Geometric torsos, trapezoid thighs, serial taches over synchronised canes. It's a fixed-smile drill for a Soviet newsreel. The marching Charlies radiate fragments of Russian typography that blast the local shops with exclamation marks.

– Make way for the Cine-fist!

And Lydia? Her eyes are drawn to the prow of the boxcart prophet cleaving towards time future. His chin points beyond the Duke to a world no longer ruled by the bullies of the Artistic Pictures Production Company. Cornfields ripple in the sun and ballet dancers perform beside them without charge. Machinists in tailored workwear thank each other for their labours. Kindly teachers issue cakes and scented soap, instead of homework to Pioneers. Lydia strolls through neat streets, spurning dust to win the prize!

– Arise ye pris'ners of starvation! Free the spirit from its cell!

Can any retelling of an event be more than more or less true?

The leading film directors are ladies and there are prominent notices for Lydia's flicks in all the popular magazines. Kingpin commissars vie with poets to escort her to private views at neoteric galleries. In hospitals powered by solar glass from Petrograd, professors of socialist medicine sprout firm limbs from stumps.

– The earth rises on new foundations.

Penitent employers pay hands and domestics tenpence, no, they bestow at least one shilling and sixpence an hour to all their permanents. Trafalgar Square is packed, cheering Lydia's programme. Someone gives her a bouquet of flowers.

– 'Tis the final conflict, let each stand in his place.

– It's humbug, Lydia, materialist humbug.

Tom wants to return to the bar.

– As a practical way of running Russia, something may come of it.

She isn't listening.

– As a faith Bolshevism is a threat to the spirit of Europe.

Lydia is standing shoulder to shoulder with the orator. Together they raft the springtide of history. The longings of a rising people swell their ragged sail. Messiah-like, operatic, his arms extend, enfold, release. He gathers his people together, he comforts them, he sets them free. When the lumberman puts his arm around the female comrade by his side, red Lydia flushes redder.

Tom prattles on.

– The temper of England is not revolutionary.

The street tilts. Tom sprawls. Street cinders rend his hands. The moon bloods, stars fall.

– Tom, Tom! Are you all right, Tom? That brute selling papers tripped you. I'm sure it was deliberate!

The speaker's forefinger spears through the lamplight towards the hotel. His fist pounds the surface of a table high above their heads.

And that's me, banging on the wall again.

OBSTRUCTION

The meeting bunches more tightly as newcomers add to the press. Young men perch on the windowsills of the two opposed hotels. The backside of the crowd seals both entrances shut. Heels rattle their doors. Whitstable's high street is replaced with back-projected stills of Kremlin skylines and Berlin tenements.

– The hypocrites gather at the memorial once a year. We shall remember them, they say. This is an emblem of our freedom, they say. For the rest of the year they avert their eyes from the dead and turn away from us. Keep your paper flowers, I say. We want a job for every poppy that you lay on that plinth. Remember that next time you take wreaths to our cenotaph, you unchristian councillors sousing in the Butcher's saloon.

I was told later the angry young man's voice could be heard from the Naval Reserve public house, fifty yards away.

It's possible. There was next to no traffic back then, no wail of extractor fans, no karaoke, no cover-bands or pummel drum and bass from passing empeethrees.

To test the claim I stood on the steps of the Duke of Cumberland Hotel at 4am one Monday morning. I shouted extracts from this book to an insomniac performance artist in period dress – a thin coat and knitted hat, cheap flats – as she walked backwards up the empty high street. No one complained except the two rough sleepers by the cash point. Slang monologues, heated rows, words taken out of context are common at the Cross in the early hours. Yes, it's certainly possible.

– Clear as a cadet kissing a bugle it were. I heared his voice a hundred yard an' more off. The buggers in the Duke din't like it, oh no. The council were dragging its feet an' he laid hard strap on 'em. I won't ever forget what he said about the poppies an' the wreaths. Keep your dead plants, he told them. I knowed they wouldn't take that lying down.

Shaving with a shaking hand just before the speech, the young man had cut his cheek. It is a scab, not a flaw, that I see in the photograph by my door. The knees of his Sunday pants shine like slicked hair in the lamplight.

– Inside the Butcher's, buying their whiskey with our rent money, that's where you find the elbow-crookers. The elbow greasers, we're out here, our traps dry and our pockets empty. In there, with the elbow crooks, it's champagne and Criterions, birds' milk and pampered paunches, bunks cosy as buttered bacon. There's no butter nor bacon on the table in Albert

Street. There's no meat in our soup, no coals in the scuttle. When mother shakes the biscuit tin it don't rattle anymore.

The lament is paired with a shot of a rectangular biscuit tin with a scratched image of Canterbury Cathedral on the lid. When the container is opened and upended, crumbs fall on to a child's outstretched hand. The infant palm swells into an adult fist squeezing a lemon. Juice pools on to sugared pancakes. A young boy in a sailor's suit claps excitedly. A street door opens, spilling light on to a pavement. The boy emerges. He dispenses the pancakes to children at the protest in the Cross. Smiling faces multiply and fill the screen.

– That's why we are gathered here tonight. To oppose reductions in wages for the miners and the railwaymen (loud applause). The time has come to act. What are we waiting for? All Russia has risen. Are we to be the last? (a few cheers). Not a penny off the pay (loud cheering). We call on Whitstable urban district council to provide work for every unemployed man of the town (applause). At tenpence a hour (cheering and shouts of that's the rate for the job). Not a penny off the pay. An tenpence an hour for the wall.

Stationed in each angle of the Cross, police officers wait for a signal. As the bluebelly blocking the junction with Terry's Lane struts back and forth he spins the truncheon looped to his right wrist like a propeller. Spin and catch. Spin and catch. He's ready to roll.

– Champing at the bit he were, that rozzer. Right champing.

An automobile butts and lurches through the crowd. It had great iron teeth. It devoured and brake in pieces. Its horn sounded, a mouth speaking.

The driver is set on reaching the front door of the Duke. Jeering and booing, the throng makes way. Two men are standing on the running board of the car. The first, in a belted greatcoat and large felt hat, is shouting. He waves his arms. The second flaps a union jack.

– Obstruction. It's obstruction I say.

– Get indoors Slawson. Let him through.

Second time in half an hour. He's looking for trouble.

– I have demands too. I demand free passage along the highway. I demand the rule of law. I demand the police take action. Sergeant, it's time you flushed these partridges from the Cross.

– Times are changing. Yourn is running out Slawson.

– Stick one on 'im!

– Sir, madam, it may be wiser to watch from inside.

Thomas and Lydia are coaxed back into the Duke by the waiter. He locks the corner door as the saloon breaks into song.

– Keep right on to the end of the road.

– Hahahaha.

– Better safe than sorry, sir, madam. It could get nasty out there.

Outside the sound of riot, indoors ill-managed merriment.

Lydia whispers something to Tom, who looks in my direction. She approaches.

– You've been watching me for the last half hour. I'm flattered. Should I be?

– You're the looker, Lydia. A picnic for the eyes.

Follow through. Go on.

– When you've finished with the book, why don't you return it to me instead of Tom? My room's over the road.

Instantly I regretted my words. Her face stiffened. I had the impression of a steel curtain coming down and blotting out the real woman. Without a word, she turned and went swiftly up the stairs, whilst I stood like an idiot gaping after her.

Is that borrowing or theft? When Stern helped himself, he said it was neither.

– We have not borrowed, we have been quickened, and we become bearers of a tradition.

Behind me the front door is breached by the two friendlies from the car. The barricade is rebuilt.

– Bloody Bolsheviks. Trash of the town.

– Toys of the Jews.

– It's treason and Twiggerism out there. We should string up that red from Ramsgate.

– That's the prickly fellah, Mr Slawson. He's been driving to the front door every half hour to show them who's in charge.

– What's Twiggerism? It doesn't sound Russian.

– Twigger is a miner, sir, a Communist with a large following. He's not out there tonight. That's a Labour meeting.

Removing his greatcoat by the door, the publican briefs his besieged regulars.

– I think we have given the officers sufficient grounds for a charge. A clear case of obstruction. A harridan from Gladstone Street stood in front of the radiator as we advanced. We tanked our way through. The bitch yowled as we rammed her. It won't last much longer. They're spouting damned nonsense about poppies and jobs. Insulting our glorious dead. Mend the sea wall with a sword in one hand and a trowel in the other. Ranters. Roundheads. Poppycock and treachery. I will not have it on my doorstep.

He shouts through the legs of the upended table.

– Damyata hell, all of you.

The cartoon panels of the door bulge and strain, the windows belly like bubbles. The swelling wood starts to split, spitting splinters. Slawson roars, a British lion. Oaaaaaarrderrrrr. The door is restored. The publican licks his teeth and tosses his mane. The saloon applauds and whistles. Cubes of red meat roll at his feet.

– The governor's pissed on their parade!

– Fix bayonets!

A middle aged woman, noosed with pearls, drawls loudly from her wingback chair.

– My humble people who expect nothing. Whatever happened to them?

Her companion laughs. He is standing on a table in evening dress, whiskey in one hand, fishing rod in the other. He sways as he monitors the clearing of the street from a window light. Below him indistinct forms thud against the frosted glass as if blundering through fog. Some men cower. Some spin away and shout.

– Hold the line! Don't be provoked!

– Steady, the Buffs!

– Strike again! Here is my arms, my head, my cheeks.

– That way, move, move!

– Remember, proletarians!

The demagogues are led away to a slammer in Bexley Street.

– They are being humbled now, my dear. Spartacus is having his collar felt. The councillor is in custody. So are his sidekicks. Jolly good. Ten minutes that shook the world, that's all it was. The mobocracy is being dispersed.

The prickly fellah bends a half-bow, twice.

– Lady Dimsdale, Sir John. Good evening to you both.

The couple wave back vaguely from the apex of the Duke's clientele. Their titles and the minor acts of recognition they bestow – a nod, a splash, a word – are highly prized by the tippling widows, surplus officers and bibulous tradesmen installed at the tables mustered in the bar.

– Take my arm, sir.

– Let me take the rod your nibs.

– Steady as you go.

– This way.

Sir John is rotated, half a brogue at a time, to face us. He doesn't spill a drop. As he sways, clock high, we anticipate a speech, perhaps a nosedive to the floor.

– That, gentlemen, is our Fisher King.

The director breaks a long silence.

– Heal him and you heal Albion, restoring fertility.

– Come again?

– King Arthur. The legendary grailway.

– Back before Beeching.

– What?

– Looks like a lost cause.

Slawson buttresses the baronet, one hand at his elbow, the other at his wrist. Davey stands short leg, ready for the catch. Dimsdale waves them both away. He clasps his hands behind his back and coughs to clear his throat.

– Order is being restored outside the ramparts. (Extended cheers and whistling.) They are reliable men, our local constabulary. Not like the turncoat Scousers. (Laughter, some booing.) Am I right to expect they will join us later? (Affirmations.) I propose that we pass round a hat to set up their drinks. For a successful assault on the enemy's position. (Hear, hear.) Slawson, get my homburg. I intend to use my own titfer for the kitty. (Cheers and applause.)

Dimsdale is helped down from the table and steered into a chair. Slawson fetches the hat from an exclusive hook behind the counter. Sir John drops a large silver coin in the crown. The saloon huzzahs.

In July 1921, at the magistrate's court in Canterbury, Councillor Johnson and Mr Hawks of the Labour Party were fined five shillings each for obstruction of the highway at the junction known as the Cross outside the Duke of Cumberland Hotel in Whitstable.

As the genteel collection bucket nods its way slowly along the bar – Bates of Jermyn Street revolving on its silk hoarding – a lighting technician is being conveyed from Sergeant Winchell's office at Paddington Green to a holding cell in the basement.

– I'm telling you, she was like that when I got there.

– You told us you didn't go in sir.

– I mean she must have been. That's why she didn't answer the door.

– Do we look like the Keystone Kops? It was your healing hands what done her, Roscuro.

– It's time for supper. Lock him up.

There is a theatrical backcloth behind their words and actions, a reviewer points out in *The Times*.

The sense that the policemen they are acting are not policemen as they really are, but policemen as an indulgent tradition has chosen to think they are, will not be banished.

It's a good point, clumsily expressed.

Winchell doesn't agree. The blue lamp over the station door sputters and pops.

Thomas is jotting something in a notebook. I need to check the archive. Brown, pocket sized, a yellow label on the front cover. I haven't seen that one before. If it has survived, it's probably in the States. Four men in leather coats, burly and breathless, enter and approach the pumps. The first one rubs raw knuckles. Another licks a split lip.

– My shout. Bitter all round?

– Shandy.

– Shandy.

– Shandy.

All about us in this town, the thirst, that thirst which is instilled into us at our creation, and which never leaves us.

A seer enthroned amid wineskins beckons to Tom with the rim of his glass.

– You'll think this place is Bedlam in Baghdad.

– Not at all. I imagine today is exceptional. A choppy night in the bay.

– I'm Perks. In property. If you are looking for a furnished flat, come to me.

– Stern. Lloyds. If ever I do, I will.

– The black nag? The geegee with the gloves? Oh, she's a winner she is.

Rising and raising his bony fists, Perks spars in the air. He whinnies and throws a few jabs. Bosh bosh. Bosh bosh. Losing his balance, he pitches on to the table. Tom helps him back to his feet. Beneath his duds the man is skeletal. His back is hollow. Rickets? Perks flops back into his seat, reedy forearms bared.

– Racing and the ring. What's life without 'em eh?

He pauses, toying with a cigar and lighter.

– Whitstable's not usually like this Stern. The last few weeks have been dreadful. The poverty of those men and their families cannot be denied. The reds exploit their pain, of course, but the hardship is real and the rot is rising. If you're a shopkeeper or a landlord, higher rates or a community with empty pockets is no choice at all. They're both poisonous for trade. The shopkeepers are in dry dock, you'll not meet many here tonight. As for the miners and the railwaymen, that dispute is a very different matter. Those brigands are holding us to ransom. We can't cave in to them.

He slaps the edge of the table.

– We won't cave into them.

– These are troubled times indeed, Mr Perks.

– And that's not the half of it. To cap it all, Whitstable's Labour Party is beating a drum for temperance. I ask you. Moderation, yes, that's the proper thing undoubtedly. Drink within your means, that's only common sense. The men shouldn't be permitted to put ale before rentbook, bread or brood. But more regulation? Prohibition? It doesn't work in your Yankee Doodle and we don't want it here. Do the socialists mean what they say, that's the question. I'm glad to say I doubt it. One of them used to run the Saracen's Head in Canterbury, for Christ's sake. It's just a tactic. They are wasting their time. They'll never see power.

– Temperance is not the issue tonight I understand.

– Quite so. The unemployed men in greatest need, those with families, were set to work on the sea wall. The usual remedy. At a rate of pay the council on its own could not afford. We were promised funds from London but Whitehall reneged on us. So we must fend for ourselves. With Bolsheviks hammering at the door of the Duke! We must stand firm. It's time for firmness, you agree?

Perks nods into the stink of his funker, squinting through blue fumes for Tom's reply.

– I feel the blackest gloom, Mr Perks. I have contempt for every existing political party, and a deep hatred for democracy.

– I say Stern. That sounds like fighting talk.

Perks throws two limp jabs from his seat, guarding his face with his left.

– The massenmensch will bawl and hustle. They will vote without reason.

– Absolutely, Stern. No question.

– Are they Greeks? No. Are we Troy?

– What's that?

– I should add, Mr Perks, that my own beliefs are held with a scepticism which I hope never to lose.

– I don't follow you.

– We need to define precisely who our enemies are.

Stepping into the centre of the saloon, Thomas points to me and shouts.

– Meddler! Snooper! Stalker! If she dies, if Fanny is dead, her blood is on your hands. You, not I, will be held responsible. Stay away from me.

He saw me and recognised me and called me out.

The bar falls silent. Oily domes, gell mops, cloche hats, shaveheads, they all turn my way. Beanies, weaves and bobs too. Behind them a pince nez and eye patch square up over a stool, fighting to get an eyeful of whatever's being looked at. Our spat is being filmed on raised phones. I've no idea how to return Tom's grass-scorcher. He has served an ace.

I get to my feet. Plaits, perms, even the ponytails back away from me.

– OOOh, a smack-up

– Chopsocky! 'Old his coat

– Settle it outside sir.

Captured by an overhead camera, I am the still pupil of a widening eye. A reverse zoom surrounds my wispy poll with bloodshot carpet tiles.

Lydia places a hand on Tom's outstretched wrist.

– Let it go Thomas. Please. Not here, not now.

Tom lowers his arm slowly.

– Sit down with me. Come.

Well done Hayward. When did she return to the fray?

– Good in here, innit.

– I'll say. Like being at the theatre.

– Bit of a letdown. Other fellah forgot his lines.

I sit for a few moments with my eyes closed. Lydia and Thomas are talking but I can't separate their words from the babble. I stand. I cup both of my ears. I infiltrate their lines. As the conversation becomes more distinct, the dialogue streams beneath the optics.

A TRINITY PILOT ROOMED HERE

– A Trinity pilot roomed here last year. The captain of a small ship. I'm told he took his own life upstairs. A sad story.

Lydia exaggerates a shudder. Tom nods. It happened when he was in Cliftonville. He'd seen an account in the local paper. The captain had placed a belt around his neck, buckling himself to the bedhead.

Am I in that room? In the same cot? Conan will know.

All his life the captain had expected death by water. He foresaw it. He was blind to it. Once, as he darned the Channel, a lowly lookingtuber told his commander he had the captain in his sights.

– You think we have eels to spare? Get out of here. Find me a target that will be missed.

In recent years the old man had rehearsed his options. Over the side, full fathom five, in the next gale? It would put the crew in danger. They would attempt a rescue. Scuttle the ship and lock himself below? A cruel loss for the owners. Lock down the crew and jump? They would be rescued in the shipping lanes. That might work.

He's still rehearsing two hours before his death as Tom joins him on a public bench at Reeves Beach. Razor. Belt. Cleaning fluid. Tonight.

– She wants me back. I won't go back.

– That we have in common.

– I provide. There's money. She will not want.

– I work in a bank. I don't want to any more.

They talk tides. The captain describes the local currents. A small anticyclonic eddy. The seep of the Swale. Tom mourns Lycidas, Ludwig and Phoebas. He dates their watery graves. The *Titanic* and the *Lusitania*, those were a dialogue. Wilton, the soccer boss slaked in Lake Gourich, he was summoned by the captain. As were thirty six drenchers lost with the Rowan. Strangers until that night, the two men share the pull of the whelming tide. So sank the daystar As they walked back into town the owner of a pirate radio station flubbed unseen in the sucking waves The captain had decided on a belt.

– It was September. When he topped himself. The old salt. Up top.

Tom and Lydia have been interrupted. A swiller in a sports shirt has timed his tackle well.

– I thought a little later in the year.

– September. Just after the hop festival. A disagreement with his better half. And money worries. The usual endgame. We've all been through one ain't we darling? No need to coil the rope and clock out is there? Not when there's bars like this and girls like you.

As news of the captain's death broke, Thomas had been on the seafront at Margate. Speculation strolled along the promenade, scattering a trail of card games and carpet dances in its wake, scam sweethearts and sly swindlers, moments of weakness distended into weeks of indulgence. Pot-slinging wags in Thanet scorched the Whitstable kettle black.

– Is there no moral high ground on the north Kent coast?

– A bluff here and there, of a crumbling kind.

– There are no cliffs at Whitstable.

– It's a low lying town.

– Washed by cockney effluent.

– Shameless shitstable!

An ash sky over a grey sea, the shriek of a train behind. Daytrippers stream from the station to overflow the trams. Later they pour from the trams to flood the station. Margate's tidal flows are regulated by the railway.

– A rather queer place. We don't dislike it.

Newsprint contorts, slapped out of shape by the gusts cuffing the shelter. Grips tighten, thumbs blacken, sheets fold and double into wads. A man in a rumpled suit settles next to Tom.

– Den of impurity, that town up the coast.

His fingernails are broken. Tom nods but doesn't reply.

– Their souls are bottomless pits.

Fingernails crabs closer.

– Pits filled with lust.

Then, in a low voice.

– Bangtails bold as brass, some of them. Those ladies make ends meet all right. Ever been to Whitstable?

Tom continues reading.

– A short ride on the train.

Tom's eyes stay locked on the page.

The tout selects another bench, a new prospect, facing the trams.

– Seen the paper? No morals up the coast, eh?

Thomas watches foys and hoys, littered nutshells riding the tide.

A punt slops in the Cherwell. Fast track Fanny auditions for the part of Mrs Stern. She's a pouter and a giggler, quick witted, with an itch to write. Thayer's gramophone horns a ragtime rhumba through their first kiss. Tom's want stems, snared in his truss. They met in April. They were married in June.

How many sweet thoughts, how much desire, led them to the grievous step.

During the war Fan had attended Dulwich House School at an outpost in Margate. Together they searched for the building. They didn't find it. They caught a train to search again. I haven't found it either.

– The square, I remember this square. We sang in the theatre.

– Did I tell you Ez has cut the Broadway and the minstrel songs? Fresca's missing. He's hacking away at my women. He has snipped out the photos. The grail survives but the music hall, it's gone. He may be right. I think he's right. In any case, it's done.

– I liked the singing.

– I must let my poem go.

– It's not you anymore. Not yours.

– He's pounding me to pieces.

– Ezra has a nose for what's coming, Tom. For what's now.

– His pencil gives me the blues.

– You're not alike, you two. Not at all.

– He has no awareness of eternity.

– Look at me, Tom. No, don't turn away. The despair of the washed-up captain in his rented room, you are never going to feel that. Never. Because I am here with you. Always. Except for the times I can't be, of course. And then I am too but in a different way. You do know that, don't you?

– The deal was sealed in Paris. Publication, payment, a prize. The swag's in the bag but the poem ain't ready. Bloody Ez.

– I think you're tired. Let's go back to the station.

– But your school…

– Let the past stay where I buried it.

Tom's eyes close on the foys. I'm leaning against the plinth of a lifeboatman a few yards away. Corked and souwestered, he shades his eyes with a bronze hand, scanning the waves for drowners. I squint along the crescent of sand pointing at the glass hangar of the Turner Contemporary.

Wouldn't it have been better for Fanny, for them both, if Tom had stayed longer at the clinic in Lausanne? Or if he had taken the job at Harvard? Pointless thoughts, meaningless speculation. Don't go there. Stick to what actually happens. Follow the spondulicks. That's the job in hand. Do what the contract with the business network states. No more, no less.

I hear the rattle of the crowded tram for Cliftonville, the bells, the fiddles, the strum of strolling musicians, flurries of sales patter unwelcome like rain, the chatter of the promenade. Dreamland's scenic railway, the pause and oh that plummet, scream I couldn't help myself my goodness me. Beach pastors, psalms, squeezebox hosannahs, player pianers, Galilee and gaiety. They ain't Jawbreakers matey they're gobstoppers. Valentino's on at The Parade, we hit town last night for the first time, a woman runs a terrible risk. Cameos, turns, curls for the cutting room floor. Fragments in Tom's notebook. No way to connect them. What a mess. What a breakthrough.

Ale swirls in fleshy drains. Back in the Duke of Cumberland, Lydia has been approached by a man in a T shirt proclaiming LET ME WASTE YOUR TIME.

– So how's the film going luv?

– Ay ay, Will's on pussy prowl.

– No chance there.

Lydia is polite. It was very kind of him to ask but no, she doesn't. That would be wonderful for someone, but no thank you not for me. No, she doesn't know if Lord Northcliffe will close the *Literary Supplement*. The raids are all rebuffed.

Turning towards the blaze, left hand plunged in a pocket, Thomas rubs his wedding ring against his thigh trying to slide it off. The band resists. He pinches the hidden hoop with his free hand. It raws over the knuckle and drops on to coin.

His ring finger feels lighter. It throbs like a lie.

As he watches Lydia chatting with Conan, he eavesdrops on the conversation of the shandy club.

– Thomas Hardy loved his wife. After she'd croaked.

– Hurhurhur.

– Y'mean Emma blue peeps, mare of Casterbridge?

– Hurhurhurhur.

– Woman much missed, how you call to me, crawl to me.

– His timing was off, old Jude the Obscene.

– Never liked him meself. The man lacked principle.

– It was all down to guilt. An' needless guilt, romantic guilt, led to rotten poetry. Way I see it, he should've ended things sooner.

– How d'yer mean?

– One, the thrill had gone, obvious. Two, they were always scrapping, hammer and tongs, all the time. No argument about that. Three, you only live once don't ya? He shooder given her the push years before.

Thomas walks over to the table. He gives the last speaker a long manhug. After kissing the man on both cheeks, pumping the hands of his three friends, and pinning imaginary medals to each of their chests, Tom circles the group clapping loudly. He punches the air, encouraging other customers to add to his applause. Some do, briefly, eager to join in with anything. Some do, awkwardly, not wanting to be left out. What had they missed?

The leather coats aren't pleased.

– Very funny mate. Now jog along.

– Beat your feet.

– Bounce.

Is Tom losing the plot? Later he said no, just developing it. He'd liked what he'd heard. Fanny often praised Thomas Hardy to needle him, quoting from poems that were merely emotional. She admired Hardy's popularity and sales. He'd set the bar.

– It was just an aside. I thumbed the ring from the toe of my pocket and put it back on.

– Lydia would have clocked it already.

– Of course she had.

REMEMBER MY PAIN

For as long as the shades stay visible I record, I describe, I transcribe. Between shots I edit and check for sources online. As I lift my glass, condensation mizzles from the base across my notes. Words magnify and melt in inky pools.

A black glove slaps against my upper arm. A duel?

– You are foraging for stories that catch the temper of our time. Is that correct? If you are competent in your craft, I may permit you to tell mine.

Her voice banishes the hubbub and the walla walla. Tom will have to look after himself. Beneath a broad black hat with a black crepe ribbon a sombre coat shrouds a hueless dress. She wears mourning pearls. Her flesh is grey, like a waning raincloud. Lady Dimsdale's darkness is the beach against which the surging colour of the saloon beats. She moves round to sit in front of me.

– My situation is common gossip in this town for a number of years, all the way through to the next war in fact. After that I am quickly forgotten.

– It is, I mean it was, a tragedy. I'm so sorry.

– What have you to be sorry about? There is only one person to blame, my husband, Sir John Holdsworth Dimsdale.

– Can you explain what happened and why?

– At midnight on 11 April 1923, a Wednesday, he will visit me for the last time here at this very hotel. We live apart. We live apart as I drink to excess, I am able to acknowledge it now. He is staying at the Bear and Key there behind you. I have rooms upstairs. We have become friends again, as one does eventually. From time to time we wave to one another from our windows. My husband wants to talk about money. He is neglectful of me – miserly, one might say – despite his substantial holdings in Jamaica. We spent the war in the West Indies. John held an appointment in fuel. I will be unsympathetic. It is the only way to treat him.

– Why's that?

– He is always trying to reduce his support for me. That's why. I believe there were times he would have preferred me dead. I am sure there were. Men are so egotistical and centred on themselves. Most especially baronets, I find. I dismiss him. The following morning, after receiving a telephone call from the bank manager – they are acquaintances, keen anglers – he will walk to the old church in Seasalter outside the town. Why there, I do not know. He kneels in the grass beside the gate. He shoots himself with a revolver. He fires upwards, through his mouth.

– How awful.

– He had threatened to do it many times before. When he was cross he would threaten it but I took no notice. Then he did.

– I don't know what to say.

– I expected questions. There are many lines of inquiry to pursue. The coroner said there was no singeing to John's moustache. How could that be? The cause of death was laceration of the brain. I was told there was a star shaped wound in the top of his head. Why then was there no hole in his hat?

– I don't know.

– The doctor said if John had been standing they would have found him on his back. He was face down. So the baronet died on his knees. His last thoughts, I am sure of this, were about the bank. His lack of credit, his loss of standing with the manager, not me. His finances were low. Our finances. A clerk had scrawled two letters, NS, not sufficient, over a cheque for nine pounds. For my husband, Sir John Holdsworth Dimsdale, a cheque dishonoured was a man dishonoured, a disgrace to England. Holdsworth held very little of worth as it turned out. I hear the awful news here, sitting at this very table, later that evening. The news of his death.

– How shocking. I can't imagine how that felt.

– I am certain you cannot. He neglected to leave a letter. Typical John. Instead of an explanation, he left debts. It will be a uniquely unbearable experience. Losing my husband in the trenches, as he led a charge to save the country, that would have been far, far preferable. Lesser women have recovered from that. My misfortune, inflicted by my husband and exacerbated by his family, exceeds theirs. I live full board in this hotel. I have no house to go to.

– Is it correct that people who saw the body thought he was resting?

– I thought it was someone asleep so I didn't disturb him. I didn't hear no shot.

– No one approached the body until later that afternoon your worship.

– Feller like that might say you was a robbin' him. Got a temper too.

– Is that something he did? Snooze out of doors?

– It is beyond my powers to explain the behaviour of the uneducated.

– Let him sleep it off I thought.

– And you, Lady Dimsdale, how do you cope?

– I continue living here, in this hotel, during the weeks that follow. I am humiliatingly dependent on the dwindling support of friends. Conan, the assistant manager, finds overpayments in my past account. He remained true. I live as a pauper. Before long I am practically in pawn, and without a penny in the world. When I have only nine shillings and ninepence left, I reach the end of my tether. I cannot go on. One morning, as daylight breaks, I walk into the sea. I try to sink. The waves wash me ashore. Three times I try to sink. Three times I fail. I long for my husband's revolver. I am quite broken. I give myself up to the police. I confess to attempted suicide.

– There are reports that a local woman helped you. She gave you dry clothes? And you escaped through a window?

– I don't recall.

– I don't mean to upset you.

– I will not shed tears in public.

– There's one thing I must ask, if I may?

– Do your job.

– That morning. Was it a serious attempt to kill yourself?

– The question is impertinent sir. Treat the lady, my wife, with more respect.

– I'm sorry. I thought you were dead. Please continue Lady Dimsdale.

– I try to find suitable employment, but I have never worked. In my first position I am denied a bath and prevented from powdering my face. My friends and supporters fall away, one by one. The estate is very small. I cannot live on the annual interest. Thirty shillings a week! I disbursed far more on jolly evenings here. I teach girls in America. Dull, so dull. I return to London, to the Great Western Hotel at Paddington Station. I resolve to sink no further. I poison myself with Lysol, a disinfectant, in room sixteen.

– I have been there. To the very room.

– Lysol burns one from the inside out. Doctors assault me with a stomach pump but I carry the day. In my bag there is a poem I have copied on to notepaper. 'They are not long, the days of wine and roses.' Indeed, they are not.

– I read those lines aloud as I stood by the door. I do wish things had turned out better.

– Thank you for that. That's very kind. I do believe it has helped a little. I've had so many wonderful evenings in here, you know. Such fond memories. Young flappers teaching me dances. Ladies' billiard matches. John up on a table, on election night, croaking his way through Jerusalem. Mr Slawson singing about cactus thighs. And now my sand is sinking. I must retire.

The scene stealer stands, extending a wraithlike hand towards me. I don't know whether I am meant to take it or shake it or kiss it, so I give her an awkward wave. She recedes slowly.

Thomas has noticed us talking. His eyes follow Lady Dimsdale through the parting football shirts. Swing doors transition the scene, four words on each, two wipes from right to left.

EVERY HEART IS CLOSED

TO EVERY OTHER HEART

– It's time. Hurry up, please. It's time.

Thomas laughs. Cut to the view from a second storey window. It's half past nine. It's dark outside. The Sterns are playing chess. Inebriated cockneys totter past Crawford Mansions and into Homer Street. Their shouts spiral skywards, curving into the rented rooms. Fanny parries them, one by one, with antiphons.

– You yercunt, yerronfer tomorrer?

– Daddy you can count on us. We'll be waiting.

– Goonight an gooriddance

– An goonight to you too, my sweet mucker.

– Larrik agin 'baht sixish faceache

– It's pillow time dearie, the sandman's waiting.

– Off nah fuckyerall

– Bottoms up boys, and boner nochy.

She flicks Tom's bishop aside then sweeps all the chessmen to the floor.

– It's time. Hurry up.

As Tom kneels to retrieve the pieces I recall the tweedy vowels of a grammar school English teacher. The elbows of his sentences are patched with leather.

– In the aftermath of war, the traditional sources of authority were weakened. The modernist cut-up, the medley of competing voices reflects this. Unattributed voices, a patchwork of quotation. What holds this poem together and how? You boy.

I grip the inkstained lid of a varnished desk. I remember carved initials with my thumbtips. I nose the teen odours of a 1970s classroom. I yawn the memory in.

– Nothing sir. Nothing holds it together. Isn't that the point?

– That's the workshy answer. Make an effort boy.

A bell in the corridor.

– It's time.

A library is closing in London. Stock is returned to the shelves.

They must know by now. You all must know. You do know, of course. Who could not know by now?

Did he realise, I wondered, how closely the halter was being drawn around his neck?

Here in the Duke it's flop time. I walk across to Tom and place a hand on his shoulder. He turns.

– Am I under arrest?

– Town like this, a line or two of greek blue yes, they might lock you up.

– I'm aware of that.

– You should get *Ulysses* back. Let me carry it.

– Good idea. An arrest for obscenity would be the death of my mother.

– There's far worse than that hanging over your head.

– You think I've forgotten?

– No, but...

– I can't call back yesterday. I've crossed a frontier. Done something that cannot be undone. There's no need for you to dwell on it.

– I'm concerned.

– Don't worry about me. I'm not going to end my days dangling.

– Or in the can?

– How's your room? Is it anywhere near that bloody sign?

– Directly above it. I've got earplugs, I'll be fine.

– A bear with a key on its shoulder. What's that all about?

– Teddy is the town burglar. He has a skeleton for every room.

– Two drunks with keys, that's what we are.

– I'm tired Tom.

– In Dublin there were two without.

– I'm turning in.

– Prisoners dream of keys.

– You were wrong about that.

I wave a six-inch nail at him. He looks baffled.

– Take that out. No one will know the reference.

– People sometimes like what they don't understand.

– I'm whacked. Let's call it a day.

I wave goodnight to Tom with my passcard. It blurs in front of me. The shot was smeared in the edit suite to confirm that we were both tired and disorientated.

A steward walks through the vacant saloon collecting glasses. As he wipes a mantel he turns to the camera, waving us nearer. He holds up a call list and taps the next location.

THE KILLER RETIRES TO HIS ROOM

Up the stairs, unsteady, muttering as he goes, Tom stumbles through a hand held sequence.

– Is all good structure in a winding stair?

– Steady, old man. Let me help you.

– My firm foot always was the one below.

From the landing Tom spots a bonnet behind him. The maid skips past without saying a word.

– It was a punishing job. Live in, if you call it living. A day off every fortnight but only out of season. Fetching, carrying, cleaning, up and down the stairs for twelve hours with hardly a minute to catch your breath. Dirty work too, and we always had to be perfectly turned out, near on spotless. Some of our regulars were generous. Others were mean and too free with their hands. And the governor's moody turns, oh my word, he had a fierce way to him. His wife was worse. It was young girl's work. I couldn't get up those stairs today, even if Rockefeller was waiting at the top with a ring.

From my room across the road I see Tom's curtains part. As they fall back a slot of light remains. It's not wide enough for me to see through.

Tom's too stewed to read. He muffles Fanny's yelps with a pillow. Music thudders from the Assembly Room beside the hotel. The lyric has an abrupt metre. How is it so loud? And why is it permitted at such a late hour?

Head in the noose
feet through the trap,
rocking to the sound of a neck that's snapped
let's dance, bop until we drop, yeaaaaah
let's dance, bop until the drop.

The last unwilling leave the two hotels, dispersing to their dwellings.

Voices murmur beneath Tom's rug. A slate lifts and clacks in the wind.

When you goe to bed, read over the carriage of your selfe that day.

Thomas returns to the window.

From separate stations above the Cross, we witness the lunar rip and lesions of the night. Pickings and scratchings in constellation, spyholes for bobbies, ticket nips. Tom plummets upwards. A warder opens the beanslot.

The stench of prison breakfast fills the cell.

He retches.

I yell from my roost.

– In Egypt that moon is the knife of a god!

He doesn't hear me. Someone in the next room bangs a protest on the wall.

I hammer back with both fists until the knocker concedes. I go back to the window. Tom has disappeared. If I were him I don't think I could sleep.

I dismissed him from my mind, and returned to the contemplation of my own affairs.

TAP AT THE DOOR

I will… examin myself every evening before I go to bed (besides praying, reading, singing, which at that time must be done also, with my family and apart), what evils have I thought, done, and spoken, and what good have I done?

Tap tap. It's the maid. She steps in quickly.

– I was wondering if I knock will he let me enter, you never know for sure do you well not me anyway. No need to worry was there darling. It was open. You were expecting me.

She giggles and places two bottles of beer on the bedside table.

– On the house.

– I wasn't sure you'd come.

– Glad to see me? Course you are. Upstanding man like yourself.

She turns and locks the door.

– Nif you ain't you soon will be. I'll see to that.

This tart's been to the movies. She thinks I'm Her Great Chance.

Joan Cade hoves close, presenting a cheek for Tom to kiss. Tom complies. She hips at his mast, then tacks away.

– I knew a man once, did a girl in. You look a safer bet. Us women take a terrible risk y'know. It will be five bob, dearie. Help me with the buttons down the back.

Thus with her great craft she caused him to yield, and with her flattering lips she enticed him.

Tap tap.

Succuba eviscerate.

– Please don't fall in love with me Thomas, may I call you Tom?

The scriptwriter takes a hanger from the wardrobe for her evening dress.

– I have brought despair to far too many. I am fond of you. I would like us to remain friends after tonight.

You and I he says, still far from wise she replies, must not commit the error, he, of falling, she, into a stormy passion

– Which enslaves us!

– Which enslaves us.

The maid looks out of the window along the high street. To screen her nakedness she holds the curtain up to her chin.

– You can always make a dress out of a curtain. That's what me mum says. It was my brother on the box out there tonight. Drew a crowd, dinny? Just you wait and see, we'll knock some fairness into this town. I'll stay for longer if you like but it costs the same again.

Tom crosses the room to stand behind her. Fud in his fingers, he kisses the top of her spine. There's something he wants.

– Can I call you Bubu? I'd like to call you Bubu.

– If I can call you Charlie.

The scriptwriter presses herself to the wall.

– There's a woman staring in this direction. From the other hotel. And there's someone watching from the window above her.

Tom bubbycup pillows his face in her hair – don't be silly, he says, there's nobody there.

Reflected in the window beside the couple we catch a glimpse of the crew. A roundel of headphones and wide eyes around a blank lens, an outer ring of tablets glowing in their hands.

– Leave that in. It works.

The director has left his seat to stand bedside the editor.

– I assume it was deliberate.

– Accidentally intended, y'know?

– A hint of retro.

– Cue eyerolls, film school eyerolls.

– All right, all right. Let's get on.

Tap tap.

The painter talks non-stop as she disrobes.

– And after you looked across at me Tom, I simply had to come over to find out if it was really you. And then that boy delivered your message. Oh, it really is you Tom, you, here in this obscure little place but the sunsets are beautiful Tom and the clouds in the water, they're a challenge, always on the move, elusive one might say, it's so thrilling that it really is you darling, really thrilling, Tom, Tom come.

Body doubles, four of them. Lipsin. Skins on skin. Wettings, firmings, widenings, cradlings. The usual hayroll.

License my roving hands and let them go. Before, behind, between, above, below. American Tom my new-found-land.

Thought felt, felt thought inked from Gill's scored plate. For a sheet he spread tongues of grass, greensward licking her flank. The fingers of the lovers interleave. His elbow and her ankle anglepoise above his head. Two fingers penetrate the frame, blessing her upturned palm with light. The illumination throws no shadows.

– Tubers and roots.

– I am the form and the hollow, the thrust and the contour.

– Percolate in copperplate, copulate in puckered bass, dance, perk perk, all night purple perk

Somedeal she sweat (tired with the game you wot). Her sweat drops bright, white, round, like pearls of Ind, her humid eyes a fiery smile forth shot.

Tap-tap-tap.

Warm rain, hot gates.

– A little bit of what yer fancy does yer good.

The screenwriter doesn't like to be bitten.

– No marks, please Tom, no marks. Manning must never know.

– I expect it to hurt a little. It's all right Tom. I know about the pain.

– No need to be shy, dearie. Look what the oysters have done for you.

The maid is muscular, with rough palms and toenails like claws.

Just looking is adultery. Thought is real and judged.

– What I want is lowbrow love, heavy knock down cave man stuff, I'm no cooing turtle dove…

Three in one, and one in three, I'm a trinal unity.

I'm a fucking machine. Tumping Tom from Trumpington.

I'm authomating. Viewing my automatism.

Look away.

Tomtom, the beating. Tom. Tom Beckett, Cranmer, Hardy, Mann. Tom Mix. With a Gunn. Tomcat. Tom Tit. Tom Codling. Tallyman, Tallis, Arne and Jones. Paine and Doubting, Hobbes and Docherty. Black Tom, Mosley, Gunn.

BAAAARP! Repetition.

Tommy rot. Tom's a toe. Peeping, Tucker, Thumb, Tit.

BAAARP!

A name, what's in a name. Any person, whether man, woman or child, may baptise an infant, in case of danger of death.

Orrow. Ahawk. As the tank engine. Me gun. Oh.

BAARP!

The breasts of the church are the two testaments; out of which we that are the children of the church suck the pure milk of the word of God.

Tomfoolery. Thomarse. Tom Aquinarse.

Here let me warre in these armes, let me lye. Here lette me parlee, batter, bleede and dye.

The convulsions were of a violence terrible to behold. Everything was confusion. A final convulsion lifted her from the bed, until she appeared to rest on her head and her heels, with her body arched in an extraordinary manner. The moments flew. Again the body arched.

If beauty is not convulsive, it is not.

And after, he thought: the sickle motion from the thighs.

And after, she thought: an angel whispered in my ear.

He grazed sleep as each dressed.

– I've a film to make, Tom darling. It's an early call.

– I'll finish my painting as the sun rises.

– I'm up first thing me duck, with work to do

Egereik. Egreeak.

All through the abandoned hours, from the dark streets flanking the hotel, sighs, lamentations and loud cries were echoing across the starless air.

United Irishmen clamour for a boat to Flushing. Napoleon will make O'Connor a General but Coigly is hanged on Penenden Heath. The stairwell blazes. In the smoke whispers of villains, of Krays, of crazies down from the smoke.

The long hair draped over his face, his Teddy Boy suit torn, a young hoodlum from London brandished a three-foot axe handle outside the Duke of Cumberland Hotel.

– We'll be back!

The yob's bottle shatters against the wall below Tom's window.

The night was as troublesome to him as the day: wherefore instead of sleeping, he spent it in sighs and tears.

A trudger lumbers to the attic landing. The footsteps sound familiar. He knuckles a door, unanswered. He raps it loudly. His portal of pleasure swings open.

– What time do you call this? Where you been?

Five minutes or an hour later, there's no way to tell which, heavy footfall drums back past the door, dopplering vertically down to the street. A lover's send-off snaps at his hammerhead heels.

– Go. Run home to her. Skit you bastard. And don't come back.

A distant slam. A matching thud above. Tom's windows rattle twice.

In the untimed dark, he studies the blur of the ceiling rose. Plaster petals. Each in his prison like Bertie, the charmer, the toff with the lot who helped himself to more.

– That arrangement worked for you, didn't it? The burden of Fanny shared.

You were given a home, a debenture, dividends, access to Bloomsbury, personal introductions, contacts that were top drawer.

– One day he will claim my ideas as his own, I'm sure of it.

– Uh? What did you say darlin'?

She throws a skinny arm, a damp rope, over his chest.

Ereek. Ereek.

Fanny's ink, blotting the daybed red.

Every man thinks of it, after.

Sinner, where can you run?

Hephaistos appears by the bed. He hands Tom a stoppered bottle.

– A salve. It will cure the wound. Rub it on the blade you used.

– Kerplupsh.

– Otto!

Tom jerks awake. His door is being kicked at, kicked at hard. It bursts open with a dazzle. Silhouettes chase shadows through the room.

– Get your strides on.

A man is pointing a revolver at him. His team circles the bed.

– You're nicked.

Tom reaches for his spectacles.

– What's your name love?.

– Joan, Joan Cade. I work here. Don't give me that look. He wouldn't let me leave.

– Anyone see the rope?

– Rope?

– Nope.

– The blade?

– What blade?

– There ain't one, gov.

– The rope he used to tie you down, miss Cade. The knife he held to your jug.

– They only pay me twelve bob a week you know.

– On yer way darlin'. Now.

The door closes, soundlessly. Sockfooted the trotabout seeks her room.

Tom locks up behind her. The nymphs are departed.

Without question numerically alone. No other besides him. Let alone any equal.

– Done. I'm glad that's over.

He smoothes his hair with programmed hands. He studies himself in the glass.

– Careful Stan, or she's going to roll off. Raise your end a bit mate.

The two orderlies remove Fanny's corpse from the apartment. The lift at Crippence Court Gardens is too small to admit the stretcher party. The tight landing and the steep stairs are difficult to negotiate.

– Let's do this one without a spill.

– Egg and bloody spoon.

– Stop wriggling missus.

Half an hour later Fanny stiffens on a slab in Paddington. Thomas, sapped, spreadeagles on a blanket. Split screen, husband and wife rest side by side.

Matrimonie, a dignified and commodious sacrament.

Tom's hair sweeps the rug. He gropes beneath the bed for the handle of the chamber pot.

And of that night we read no further.

I TRUST YOU SLEPT WELL SIR?

– I did not. I dreamed of the burial of I know not whom, and that I stood by the grave.

– How are we this morning? A sore head?

– I awaked sad.

After the last of the stopouts had stumbled home, as the fox was gutting a final black sack, the baker is the first to appear on the high street. A doughhead cycling to fire the ovens, he kneads a scoop of dream with each drowsy push of the pedal. Fishermen set course for the harbour where, leaning against the trucks and railway wagons, they share dawn gaspers with nervous blacklegs.

Waking in the attic Joan remembers everything. Last night presses its knees upon her chest like a raging monster.

In September 1922 a parlour maid at the Duke of Cumberland Hotel in Whitstable will be imprisoned for two months with hard labour. She has stolen three tablecloths and two pillow slips said to be worth £1 from Mrs Slawson, wife of the proprietor. She pawns the loot in Canterbury.

Kitchen hands encroach on basements. White collar staff stride to the railway stations. Drivers and stokers linger beneath coarse blankets, withholding their wives and their labour. Rooks roost on steam whistles, pigeons perch on static lathes, avian solidarity. The scavenger at the Cross scoops the first turd of the morning into his handcart. Supermarket lorries rumble stock to storerooms. Shelf-fillers trundle loaves and toilet rolls through empty aisles. Horseboys stir in the roofs of backstreet stables. Car doors clump as commuters, denied trains, head for the city. The shops rattle open.

Dawn was defeating the last hour of night which fled before it, so that in the distance I could see the shimmering of the sea.

Having set my alarm for five thirty I am up and in position, watching from my window for movement at Tom's. I pass the time tidying up my notes from yesterday.

Tom is roused by a babble of passengers waiting for the motor bus to Canterbury. As they gather under a side window of the hotel, noise without speech fingers his ear. His eyes unstick. As the plaster rose comes into focus, pan clang and skillet smack up the stairwell, china and cutlery clatter at the door.

– Good on yer boy!

– Soft bed and a fry were it?

– We'll show 'em again next week!

The young pair of lungs that blew from the box cart, the maid's brother, has been released. Passing through the Cross, he raises a clenched fist. The salute triggers jeers and cheers from the bus stand.

– Stand together! A fair rate.

– We're with you bro.

– Shove off to Russia.

– Hush, Billy, hush now.

– Not a penny off the pay.

– Not an hour on the day!

– Shut thy gob lass or I will do it foree.

Breakfast is a rush job at the police station on the Harrow Road. The bacon is limp and not a single yoke is dry. There's no time for pipes. Sergeant Winchell was roused before the night shift ended. The officers he named as he pulled on his shirt have lined up for a briefing.

– Yanks always make poor husbands, it seems to me. They choose badly and they exercise no control. Twelve years ago Doctor Hawley Harvey Crippen murdered his spouse, a henpecker, a loose music hall type, after she had seduced the lodger. Last night's crime has many similarities. Until recently the Sterns lodged with Lord Russell, the aristo conchie. Russell's a jailbird and a notorious womaniser. The lord and the lady are bound to have bumped. Both households, the Crippens and the Sterns, quarrelled constantly. The doctor, so-called, was fascinated by the music hall and a slave to detective novels. The man we are after today shares these cravings. The quack fled on a liner with his squeeze. Like as not Stern will try to quit the country too. There may be another woman involved. There were letters in a cupboard that suggest as much. As you know, we caught Crippen by boarding a faster ship. Well Stern's no match for Crippen. He won't make the Channel. We've a man alongside him already. We'll collar the killer today lads.

In Tom's bedroom a jug of water steams beside a bowl on a table. The constables stamp their boots and cheer in the moist haze.

– I trust you slept well sir?

What place is this? What region? Of the world what coast? Where am I? Beneath the sun's rising or beneath the wheeling course of the frozen Bear? What air is this I breathe? What soil lies beneath my weary frame? What horror do I see? With bloody murder destroyed, my wife lies slain.

Winchell waves to him from the foot of the bed.

– Catch you later Thomas Stern.

There's a sickly taste in his mouth. Bitumen with vinegar. Rubbing his face Tom pivots out of bed to uncurtain the day. A container lorry, taller than the shops it shakes, thunders through the Cross. The wheels throw up a smog of grit from which a grocer and his horse emerge. The nodding animal is harnessed to a shelved cart stocked with vegetables, bottles, tins and demijohns which it is hauling towards the hotel. An ambling march in a low octave supplies a workaday mood. Craftsmen toting grips of tools flit across the street, emerging from nowhere, tacking into alleys that funnel to boatyards. A cyclist enters screen left, wobbling into view from Harbour Street.

Laced black boots rise and fall. The cog spins as the cranks clockhand between piling trouserlegs. The links of the chain zip across the screen. Through blurring spokes we spot a pair of hi-vis trainers, yellow, topped with jeans.

As DC Janes reaches the entrance to Knots Yard, he dismounts to speak to a plainclothes officer – a young constable in a brown hoodie – who has been stationed here since dawn. From this spot you can monitor five of the Duke's exits.

– Late twenties, gent, no facial, black and stripe, a bowler and valise. No overcoat reported.

– No sign yet sir.

– Where's he off to next and how, that's what we need to know. Stay on him.

And in the morning I wished it had been evening, and in the evening I wished it had been morning and I had no rest, but trouble on every side.

Tom watches from above as root vegetables are cradled from the cart to the hotel's kitchen. There is a knock at the door behind him. His taxi will arrive at ten.

– They are hunting me down, I must move on.

Traders in aprons polehook at awnings. Earlybirds peck at displays. Brooms scratch the pavement. Caps chew over last night's collars. What's to be done? Infants totter to classes, escorted by matrons in black. The gaslamp in the Cross stands like an upturned axle. It's the still point around which Whitstable turns. Or one of them.

Janes punts his cycle towards Sea Street, heaving his leg above the saddle beneath Tom's window. A wheezing truck, hung with tarpaulin, pulls up at the garage. Three men with sacks clamber into the back. The wagon exits towards the Horsebridge. The driver raises a hand to Janes who has dismounted by the Prince Albert to instruct another observer posted at the rear of the hotel.

– Where's he off to next and how.

At the first sign our target is rising – a wave from a top floor window by a maid I'd paid to alert me, a text from another – I pull on my jacket and hurry downstairs. I nod to the desk manager, cross the road, nod to Conan, and mount the stairs of the Duke two at a time.

A voice tinkers in my ear. It will not stop.

– Sell him, sell him, sell him, sell him.

I bend at Tom's door. I can hear him speaking.

– Inescapable punishment for my wrongdoing.

He's got someone in there with him. Who?

– Blot out, o lord, as a thick cloud of night our transgressions and as a morning cloud our sins: make us children of the day and of the light.

No, he's on his own. Praying. Well, if that's what fills his nib with ink why not. An archbishop once told me that prayer is a constant movement into an endless mystery, just like a detective story.

– Always. Without ceasing. At all times.

– It does no harm. Every little helps.

– One fact leads to another – so we continue. Does the next fit in with that? A merveille! Good, We can proceed. The next little fact – no! Ah, that is curious. There is something missing – a link in the chain that is not there. We examine. We search. And that little curious fact, that possibly paltry little detail that will not tally, we put it here!

I crouch and peep again. I see Thomas in a postcard still, framed by the keyhole. He is kneeling, head bowed hands clasped, beneath the arch of a window. The reverse shot is a small eye, my eye, snared in a smaller keyhole. I blink and I'm gone.

Another peek. This time he's shaving. I step away as eggs, toast and tea are delivered to his room. I look again. Tom leafs through a morning paper. Where did that come from? It's of no moment. There'll be nothing about Crippence Court Gardens in it, no mention of Fanny or Sergeant Winchell. That's for sure.

He reaches for his notebook. I know what he's about to write. It's here in my hand. He sets the date and the time – without stating a location – at the top of a fresh page. Then the harvest begins.

Daily, a terror of eternity.

Beneath it.

The sickle motion from the thighs
Three dreams cross.

He looks out of the window towards the gaslamp.

Hire us
With pocketed hands and hidden faces
We stand about in dusty places
Defeated by pain

When I found the reworked lines in the *Selected Poems*, I marked each of them with a guillemet. In the margin I added a question – Whitstable 1922?

While I am more confident about some attributions than others, there is enough evidence to make the connection. The questions that nag at me concern Tom's reworking of the experience. Last night the faces were uplifted, soft lit, and full of hope. The spirit of the strikers was not crushed, not when they were outfoxed by Slawson, and not when they were forcibly dispersed. I guess I should make allowances. Tom's a poet after all. He has to concentrate and transmute the experience. He has to make it impersonal so it can be shared as poetry. The correlate must be objective, tradition must be respected, or the work will fail. His pen skitters across the page.

> *A sword in one hand and a trowel in the other.*
> *Here is a place of disaffection.*
> *Thought, study, mortification, sacrifice.*

He opens a window before leaving the room. He isn't surprised to find me on the landing. There is no greeting. His words are detached, and rehearsed, as if they are borrowed.

– I won't hang for Fanny. You, not I, shall quake for't.

– What?

– Last night never happened. I will deny everything.

– But Thomas.

– By stamping out passion I shall become free. I will be stone. I will shed the love of created beings.

Is he still drunk? He asks me to take his bag down to the foyer. He's off to explore the seafront.

– What did you see?

– Answer the sergeant

– An unmade bed. Milt on crumpled sheets. The impress left by bodies. A leather strap tied to the bed head.

I drop the valise at reception. I hurry towards the water after Tom.

I pass an ice works, padlocked by receivers. I glance up at the Painted Lady of Chance, lofty and impassive. Boatyards back into the estuary, some quiet, now all gone. At Reeves Beach I overtake a youngish man. He bags his face with a brown hood as I pass. Red sails swarm on the horizon. Barges breach a picket of smacks and yawls. A forge. A furniture shop. Here on the river's edge, as always, the bicker of gulls, of profit and loss, nods from joggers and dogwalkers, loneliness, ruin, regret. Is the true owner of this land, the only real survivor, the sea gull?

– Every river has two banks.

The director has returned.

– On one side, memory is washed away. On the other, the good times return.

– So which side is Tom?

Natives block the track above the shingle beach. Jackets of affluent cut command the waterfront. An operator cranks a camera on splayed stilts. Actors carry furniture into a cottage of creosote planks, stooping to enter a tiny door. Like many watching from the way, they are dressed in the workaday dud of fisherfolk. Shawls, coarse coats and heavy boots. Kohl and cream mark them out. An actress balances an upturned chair upon her head, a homely crown of wooden legs. Three men mime an argument. Bear Hayes barks orders though a horn.

– Block him. Push him back with your belly Johnny. Show some bloody concern, can't you. Cut, cut.

Lydia flaps a greeting to Tom. Snuffed, she wears stubbed brown. An actor distracts her with a query. A copper, loaned by the local station to keep gawpers at bay, spots her wave. His badged helmet revolves against a cloud. Thomas spins on his heels and heads for the boatyards.

The shoare of silver streaming Themmes. Light in the form of a river. Men werken. Hands expert with red sails.

Servicing Tom's room, Joan Cade unfastens a belt from the headrail.

I am standing roughly where he retreated, trying to identify the exact spot from stills of the film. I hold the photographs up, trying to match them to the remaining roofscape. There is no correlation. They connect with nothing. The ground is dark in front of me, and me alone. Not quite. Dogdraggers and buggyshovers detour round my shadow, crunching aghast across the shingle beach. I'm in their way.

Do I have enough, can I uncover enough, to deliver all I've agreed?

– Taken as a whole, my enquiries had yielded little. I was no nearer solving the problem I had set myself.

– You will. Stay on it.

Tom discards his shoes. His trousers are wet to the knees. The surge is muddy. He can't see Verdie. He wades deeper. The missing body stays lost until a pair of shoulders breaks the surface twenty metres out, breakfast for squabbling gulls.

– Londrowners, we call them.

I can't let this happen. Nobody wants this to happen. Not the business network paying for the project, not sergeant Winchell, Fanny, neighbours or the bank.

At the waterline a child is bailing brine with a seashell. Tom teases him.

– Do you think you can empty the sea with that?

– Sure I can mister, before you know it.

The tide reverses out at speed. Fishermen scratch their heads on yawls stranded in a vast mud flat. Fish gasp, fish flap. The miracle of kinema.

Tom returns to the path. He heads for the hotel, lecturing himself loudly. He marches to the cadence of his monotone words, halting, closing his eyes and taking a deep breath between each line.

– The complete and not the fragmentary.

– Adult not the immature.

– Not chaotic, orderly.

– Adult not the immature.

– Not chaotic, orderly.

– The complete and not the fragmentary.

– Adult not the immature.

He moves along the pavement in fits and starts.

When Tom doesn't give way in Terry's Lane, a skateboarder toes a nosegrind as a warning. He ignores her. Movover, she shouts. No response. She bails at speed, staggers backwards, and falls against a flint wall. Her flooding hair is a frothing toe. A trumpet sounds. Pfthherrrrrrthhhh.

Tom doesn't notice. His chanting is more subdued as he approaches the Cross. Is the traffic making his words less audible? The recording is poor, for sure. Perhaps he's self conscious, a little embarrassed? Without looking, he steps into the junction. Outtatheway a swerving cyclist yells. An oncoming car skids with a squeal. A van brakes, its horn blaring at the bike. A double decker bus wallows into Sea Street.

On its side, in type taller than Tom, there's an advert for a confession app.

MISERE DE MI

As the scoot train crosses the saltmarsh Thomas writes with a lurching hand.

> *We are the dead on leave. There is only one itinerary and one destination. I must return. I will return. There is no escape into the dead land, the cactus land.*

He caps the pen, returning it to his pocket. Foxtail. Bur-reed. Hornwort. A greening expanse, dyked and drained. Huts. A glimpse of teal. A church waits on the horizon.

The gravenear, gravenaying church.

The disturbance of all disturbings.

All Saints at Graveney.

John and Anne, the brass Martyns, have lain there in the nave, side by side, waiting with frowns, biding their time in silence, spurning touch, not turning to each other, not walking the dog, for more than five hundred years.

Soon a boneyard will herald Faversham.

– I could see by the expression on his face that he had little hope.

Conan made all the arrangements. After the near miss outside the hotel, he spoke with Tom privately. He called the bank in Lombard Street and switched the cab booking to the railway station. Victoria maelstrom, here we come. The newspaper boys and the hireling drivers are searching for yesterday's chalkmarks and taking up their former positions. The cow is being led back on to the platform. Chars are mopping the dancefloor at the Palais and the Palace Theatre. Marie Lloyd is sleeping in. So is Otto. Fanny is in Chelsea, shopping for chocolate to share with her spouse.

– He takes flake with his tea. Fruit and nut at supper.

Tom flicks my mystery open.

– 'Like a good detective story myself,' remarked Miss Howard. 'Lots of nonsense written, though. Criminal discovered in last chapter. Everyone dumbfounded. Real crime – you'd know at once.'

In the manager's roost at Faversham, whiskered brims are spouting song

she told 'em all she'd never 'ad
'er ticket punched before

– Hahahahahahahahaha

A warrant rests on the desk.

I look across at Tom. Last night he accused me of murder in front of a large crowd of witnesses. This morning he said that I would be punished for Fanny's death. I don't know him at all, not really. I've no idea what's going on inside his head.

The voice tinkers in my ear.

– Sell him, sell him, sell him, sell him.

– When we stop, cross the platform for the high speed to St Pancras sir.

The onboard manager is speaking to Tom. A bulky mechanism suspended from his neck emits a frieze of folding tickets fringed with orange.

– There should be time to visit the platform caff. So long as there isn't a queue. You'll have to move sharpish, mind.

Porters and passengers step aside as Sergeant Winchell advances through the station underpass, a pounce of reporters and cameras whirling about him.

– How'd yer find the killer?

– Of the three shots fired 'ow many hit her?

– Hold the correspondents here.

– How's yer angover skip?

– Marie Lloyd blow yer a kiss?

– You heard the sergeant. Step back now.

– I was absolutely mobbed. Cameras were thrust into my face and I was practically at their mercy. I refused to answer the questions they asked. Justice does not seem to weigh with these people, so long as they get copy.

Winchell clears the steps leading up to the platform two at a time. At the top he nods to a young man in a brown hood waiting by the box office. The two figures pogo as the handheld camera catches up. The snitch touches the peak of his cowl and points to the train on the right. The high speed has been sealed and delayed on Winchell's instructions. All the passengers have been held on board. As the guard unseals a door it bleeps. The sergeant enters with a digital fanfare. I'm sitting at a nearby table ready to meet him.

– Sell him, sell him, sell him, sell him.

I get out my notebook and describe what I've seen. I give Winchell the false name the killer has assumed. I report our conversations. I provide details of incriminating paintings. I hand over a list of the people Tom has met since leaving the capital.

– I John saw these things and heard them.

A pierced cheek pikey slams his tattooed palms on to the window by my head.

– Copper's nark!

I flinch. Tom turns a page as Winchell shakes my hand.

– I am pleased with you, he says. You have a good memory and you have given me the facts faithfully. Of the order in which you present them, I say nothing – truly, it is deplorable! But I make allowances – you are upset.

The sergeant instructs his men.

– Fetch him. Let's do it.

Two officers pass down the aisle to where the bankbard sits reading.

Looking up, Thomas sees the uniforms approaching.

Raising a hand he asks if they can explain the delay.

– Have you any idea what's going on, officer?

– Is it Mr Stern sir? Mr Thomas Stern?

The first officer leans across the table to clasp the murderer's left arm. The second hoists him, raising the right shoulder of his jacket so high their captive is unbalanced, right foot toeing the floor. Tom doesn't resist. He is dragged away by the two constables, hopping awkwardly between them.

– Thank God it's over. The suspense has been too great. I couldn't stand it any longer.

– That's what Crippen said, isn't it sir?

– On the Montrose. In the estuary of the St Lawrence River.

– How is that relevant sir? Have you no words of your own?

– I will confess what I know and what I know not.

– That's the spirit sir.

– It ends with a mystery which we can perceive but not finally decipher.

– This way. Mind the step now.

The hacks and the snappers have blocked the underpass. They call for facts and photographs. Tom's next words to the arresting officer are barely audible.

– He spoke very quietly, so low we were hardly able to ear 'im.

– There has been someone with me, he said.

– Stern claimed that somebody else was involved?

– Someone beside me for the last day, that's what he said.

– Yes, that was the gist of it. Then he said

– I do not know his name.

– Yes, thass correct. I do not know his name. Thass what he said.

– Trying to shift the blame is he? Well, it won't wash.

Departure times for Whitstable have been severely disrupted by the arrest. The barriers gape in the ticket hall, unattended. At the window there's no one to ask. The cab rank is empty. I check the monitor for updates.

– Take him too.

– Winchell! What's going on?

– This way sir.

At the front of the station, the rear doors of the paddy wagon slam shut. The vehicle shrinks, receding into Faversham, the nineteen twenties, memory and the can. In a wing mirror officers dwindle to smudges then spots until they're gone.

The papers retail the story for days. Killer taken at Faversham after rail pursuit. Accomplice captured. My lawyer has advised me not to say a single syllable more about the case. But there are bills to pay, legal and medical and copyright. More books to buy. Whitstable's business network is withholding my fee. Reputational damage, that's their line. They will cough up eventually but not before they've made their point.

Fanny is not at all well.

– I'm back Fan. Don't I rate a hello?

– Hello Thomas. There's chocolate by the typewriter.

Where is forgiveness to be found?

And where the certainty of unchanging love?

APPEAL

– It is impossible to aggravate the publicity and sensationalism which has surrounded this case. The country talks of nothing else.

– Agreed, Home Secretary.

Churchill pulls on a stogie, a Criterion, an Imperial No 3 with a reputation behind the name. From his desk he can see the Whitehall skyline. Slates and eaves, chimney pots, spies, an astonishing number of pigeons. Shining avalanches of guano.

– We must not fetter the accused on grounds of taste.

– Certainly not. But is authorisation without a precedent wise?

Winston uncaps his pen.

– Permission for publication has been sought on the grounds that money is needed for the prisoner's defence. The application will be granted.

Let's dance perk perk all night purple perk our last purple perkle.

Three studios compete for the rights. Five enquire about a sequel.

As the credits roll – Christie Laud, Vivienne Joyce, Don Eliot, Henry Hawley Dews, Aggie Bunyan – the audience gets to its feet. The mousetrap seats of the cinema snap shut, thuddering applause. Some shadows stretch, others duck back down for bags and coats. Phones flip open, one uplighting a yawn. In the multiplex, in the Coliseum and in the Oxford Picture House remembered scenes are shucked and shared in the slow shuffle to the bar, to cars, and the buses back home.

– So, did he do it?

– Do what exactly? Who?

– Nothing like the poster was it.

I'm tapped on the shoulder by someone sitting behind me. I turn around. It's Conan, the assistant manager from the Duke. My jaw drops. Winchell's still looking for him.

– Who is there now for me to share a joke with?

– I'm sorry?

– Do your homework lad. In the end, everything is a gag.

He sprouts a toothbrush moustache and a Chaplin smile. Then he heaves a slab with a ridged leather spine on to the seatbacks between us. I recognise it immediately.

– It's the register you were looking for. From the Duke.

– I can't take that. The police are still searching for it.

– So? Hand it in when you're done.

– How will I explain that?

He shrugs and is gone. I drag the ledger to the aisle. I splay the boards on the sloping carpet. I shovel through the leaves.

I rip out the telltale page.

It's missing.

Rain pats at the windows of Crippence Court Gardens.

There's a clack from the bedroom. It's the lampswitch. A spring groans.

Tap tap tap dink.

– Thomas.

Tap tap tap. Bellissima locomotiva. Tap tap tap dink

– Tom, are you there? I can hear bees.

Tap tap tap dink.

– What are you doing out there?

Tap tap tap dink. Tap tap tap. Going right on to the end of the line.

An environmentally friendly book printed and bound in England by www.printondemand-worldwide.com

PEFC Certified

This product is from sustainably managed forests and controlled sources

www.pefc.org

PEFC/16-33-415

This book is made of chain-of-custody materials; FSC materials for the cover and PEFC materials for the text pa